P9-DNO-216

CHASE BRANCH LIBRARY
17731 W. SEVEN MILE RD.
DETROIT, MI 48235

STREETS OF NEW YORK

VOLUME

I

FOREWORD BY
SHANNON
HOLMES

WRITTEN BY
ERICK S.
GRAY

WRITTEN BY
ANTHONY
WHYTE

WRITTEN BY
MARK
ANTHONY

WHERE
HIP HOP
LITERATURE
BEGINS...

AUGUSTUS
PUBLISHING

This is a work of fiction. Names, characters, places, and incidents are products of the author's imagination or are used fictitiously and are not to be construed as real. Any resemblance to actual events, locales or organizations, or persons, living or dead is entirely coincidental.

© 2009 Augustus Publishing, Inc.
ISBN: 978-0-9792816-7-9

Novel by Anthony Whyte, Erick S Gray and Mark Anthony
Foreword by K'wan
Edited by Lisette Matos and Joy Leftow
Creative Direction & Design by Jason Claiborne

All rights reserved. No parts of this book may be used or reproduced in any manner whatsoever without written permission, except in the case of brief quotations embodied in critical articles and reviews. For further information contact Augustus Publishing

Augustus Publishing paperback May 2009
www.augustuspublishing.com

Nothing ever just happens. You have to make it happen. There are builders and great people all around us. All you have to do is find them. Here at Augustus Publishing we have the best standing with us. We would like to say thank you to the following people, first and foremost The Duke Steven Beer, Harvey Tanton, Bill Gladstone and the staff at Waterside Productions, Tamiko Maldonado for all your help, Virginia Vaca, Joy Leftow, Lisette Matos, Robert Guinsler, Marva Allen at HueMan Bookstore, David Wilk, Divine at Books In The Hood, Brett Wright, and the staff at Uptown Magazine, Omar Rubio, Shannon 'The Don' Holmes, the great K'wan and Harlem's own Treasure Blue. We would also like to thank F.E.D.S. magazine, ASIS, Don Diva, Susan Hampstead, Jessica Silver and Shae James for contributing to the growth of the genre. And to all the real scribes out there, Arlene Brathwaite, Caroline McGill, Wahida Clark, Sharron Doyle, Brooke Green, Brandon McCalla. Jules and Nelson Ninn at Nikko, DC Bookman and DC BookDiva, thank you. To Jimmy DaSaint and The Real Freeway Ricky Ross, thank you. Ket at From Here To Fame, thank you. Thanks to the staff at Vibe Magazine, Source and Essence Magazine, B.E.T., XXL and Smooth. Judith Aidoo, Jerry Lamothe and Buttahman thank you. Nakea Murray, Linda Williams, Kaven Brown, Ian Miller, Chris Howard and the Urban Book Source thank you. Antonia Badon, you are amazing. Mr. Polifick Erick S Gray, Mark Anthony at Q'Boro, keep on. Thanks to all the readers, Bookstores and libraries around the country. Hip Hop Literature lives on. Because of your collective energy we've been able to put the fun back in reading.

foreword

SHANNON HOLMES

My mother used to always tell me, 'Boy, all you wanna do is eat, sleep and run the streets.' At an early age, she could see the transformation that I was going through. She could see her youngest son becoming infatuated with the street life and she was powerless to stop it.

Truth be told, I thought that the Streets of New York had prepared me for everything. I thought I had either done everything there was to do or seen everything there was to see. I believed that New York City was the end all and be all. To me (and other street dudes like me), it was the capital of the world. New York was definitely the center of my universe. It wasn't until I got on a real serious paper chase, selling drugs in different cities, did I see that New York hadn't prepared me for everything. There were still some things I hadn't experienced, partaken in, or seen. I soon learned that out of town cats got some shit with them too.

While I was hustlin' outta town in DC and B'more, my young eyes were exposed to many things. I placed myself in situations, life or death shit, where I had no business. With that said, I saw things that would make a grown man cry and the most heartless of killers cringe.

Here's a taste from deep in the heart of the Streets Of New York. Check it out and you'll see that this is only the tip of the iceberg...

prologue

ERICK S GRAY

Queens, N.Y. 3:35 a.m.

"You still coming through? I'm waiting for dat dick," Diamond questioned a prospective client. She was in room 226 of the Executive Motel over on the Conduit waiting for her $100 to show up.

"Yeah, I'm coming through right now, shorty. Give me like twenty minutes, ahight?" Squeeze said, pushing the 4x4 down the Van Wyck while holding the cellphone to his ear.

"Ahight," she said, chewing on bubble gum and poppin' it.

"I'm sayin' tho', you chargin' me full price tonight?" he asked.

"I gots to. My daddy is here with his bottom ho'. They both sleepin' in the room. We gots to fuck up in the bathroom."

"Damn, the bathroom, ma...? You chargin' a nigga full

price to fuck in the bathroom...? Hook a nigga up, lovely. You know wha' I'm workin' wid, look out. I ain't got dat hun'red right now," Squeeze explained.

"I'm sayin' tho', how much you gots?"

"Like eighty bucks. You good on dat?"

Diamond sucked her teeth without giving the offer any thought. She made a little over $1,200 tonight. Her pimp had her out there on the track since nine that night and she'd been on dick since then with his bottom ho'.

"Ahight, but you gots to make it quick."

"I'll be there in ten."

"You know where the Executive is at in Queens??"

"Yeah, I know where you at."

"Call me when you get to my floor, okay?"

He hung up and shouted out to his accomplices in the truck with him, "That's a stupid ho! We 'bout to get dat money, she just told me dat her pimp's sleepin'.'"

"Word?" Show asked with excitement.

"Yeah, we got this!" Squeeze reassured.

Diamond turned off her cellphone and slowly eased into the room where her pimp was sprawled out across the bed. His bottom ho' was beside him sleeping. Her Daddy, a young twenty-one year old young man had two of Queens most successful women in the pimp world, was slipping right now. He was asleep when he was supposed to be making money. He was supposed to be up on things, especially his money and his bitches, his bread and butter.

Clad scantily in her mini jean skirt and a bra, Diamond pulled out a cigarette from her purse, lit it and sat against the wall near the door and waited for her date and money to arrive. She glanced at the time. It was almost 4:00 a.m.

Outside the motel, a 2003, burgundy GMC pulled into the motel parking lot and four men stepped out into the cool night air. They glanced around for a moment and then headed for the motel entrance.

"What room she in?" Pooh asked excitedly. He was the youngest in the group, only twenty-one.

"Room 226."

"Her pimp in there wit' her? Cuz I ain't going up in there for some chump change. I need dat money," Show said.

"Nigga, the bitch been working all night. I'm telling you, if you see shorty, you know she getting dat money for her pimp— she bad," Squeeze explained. "I say about two G's or better."

"Ah, dats what da fuck I'm talkin' 'bout," Show grinned.

The Executive had a reputation for being the ho-tel where anyone can pay up to fifteen, twenty dollars per hour for a short stay. All four men slipped pass the nodding clerk inside the motel.

They took the stairs two flights up and cautiously approached their destination. 45's and 9mm's came out, the two most popular handguns people die by in the hood. The date took out his cellphone and made the call.

"What up," Diamond picked up on the first ring.

"Yeah, it's me. I'm outside," Squeeze stated.

"Okay," she answered and went to open the door.

Outside her door, their gats were cocked back and ready. They heard the door being unlocked and when it opened, they saw the bitch's face. All four men rushed in with guns drawn, yoke the bitch and tossed her to the ground. They were able to quickly restrain her but she let off a piercing scream.

Hearing his ho yell woke up the young pimp and his bottom bitch. The nigga was wide-eyed when he found himself staring down the barrel of a 9mm.

"What da fuck?" he asked in bewilderment.

"Nigga, you know what time it is. You fucked up!" Squeeze announced glaring down at him.

"Daddy, I'm sorry. I didn't know!" Diamond shouted from her hands and knees. "I'm sorry Daddy. I'm sorry!"

"Bitch, shut da fuck up cuz you bout to get yours!" The pimp was furious. His bottom ho was in tears. Show and Pooh dragged both of them off the bed and onto the floor.

"You got dat money on you?" Squeeze asked taking aim at the pimp's dome.

"Fuck you!" he shot back.

"What? Nigga, you ain't in no position right now to come out your mouth. Don't fuck wit' me! I'll body your ass right now if you want. Fuckin' test me, nigga!"

"Where da money at?" Squeeze shouted.

The pimp didn't answer. He glared at his pathetic, whimpering ho' across the room, wanting to beat the shit out of her for being so fucking careless. Without warning, Pooh rushed over to the pimp and kicked him across his face with his size 11 Tim's. The young pimp bellowed in pain, clutching his jaw as blood leaked from his wound onto the room carpet.

"Nigga, we ain't fuckin' playin'! Fuck dat!" Pooh shouted aiming the gat at the pimp.

"Nah, chill. We just tear this room apart till we find it," Promise uttered. He was the most quiet. All night he was thinking that they didn't need to go that far with the violence. "You know dat shit up in here somewhere," he said quietly.

They all nodded.

"Take your fuckin' clothes off," Squeeze demanded of the pimp.

"Y'all bitches too. Fuckin' strip, hos'!" Show yelled impatiently.

Both ho's took their clothes off. The room was searched and torn apart. They knew the money was in there somewhere. Homeboy didn't have any cash on him and neither did his hos'. Then Show smashed the television against the floor and found the dough taped behind the TV.

"Got it," he shouted.

"How much, how much?" Squeeze asked quickly joining him.

"Hold on. I'm counting it now."

His hand slipped around twenty and fifty-dollar bills. It was $2,200.

"Ahight, let's be out," Promise said.

"Nah, nah, not yet," Pooh said peering down at the naked bitches.

"What?" Promise asked bewildered.

"Bitch, come over here and suck my dick!" Show demanded.

Her eyes were stained with tears. "Bitch, you deaf? You heard what da fuck I said. Come over here and suck my dick!" Show shouted as he unzipped his pants and pulled out his dick.

The whore did as told, got on her knees whimpering, and slowly but reluctantly placed his dick into her mouth. Diamond glanced at her pimp before she started sucking.

"Um...ssshhhh...shit! Dats the fuck I'm taking about!" Show grunted.

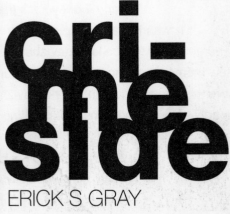

cri-me-side

ERICK S GRAY

"I ain't down for this shit. I'm out," Promise said, leaving the room and heading back to the truck.

Within ten minutes, both hos' were getting sodomized in the motel room something serious. Their pimp was tied up and placed in the corner. All he could do was bit his tongue, screaming out. He watched both his hos' fucking and sucking.

Promise woke up to the sound of Jay Z's *Big Pimpin*, blasting through his stereo system.

> *You know I thug 'em, fuck 'em,*
> *love 'em, leave 'em*
> *Cause I don't fuckin' need 'em*
> *Take 'em out the hood*
> *Keep 'em looking good*
> *But I don't fuckin' feed 'em*
> *First time they fuss I'm breezin'*
> *Talking 'bout what's the reasons*

It was his alarm indicating it was time to get his ass up and get ready for the long day ahead. He tossed and turned for a few moments, trying to drown the sound out by placing the pillow over his head but it didn't work. Jay Z's vocals could still be heard loudly. He cursed himself for setting his stereo alarm so damn loud.

> *...beep-beep and I'm pickin 'em up*
> *Let 'em play with the dick in the truck*
> *Many chicks wanna put Jigga fist in cuffs*

Divorce him and split his bucks
Just because you got good head
I'mma break bread
So you can be livin' it up
Shit I part's wit nuthin'
Y'all be frontin'...

"Fuck it!" he mumbled, throwing back the covers and rising. "She gotta get up anyway," he said referring to his company in the next room. He stepped out of bed clad only in his red, silk boxers and quickly pressed the power button on the stereo shutting off the loud rap.

We spendin' cheese
Check 'em out now
Big pimpin'
On B.L.A.D.'s
We doin' big pimpin' up in NYC
It's just that Jigga-man, Pimp-C and
B.U.N.B.
Check 'em out now...

He headed to the second bedroom and peered in at her sound asleep. She was looking so peaceful he thought he should give her five more minutes. Maybe go downstairs and make a quick cup of tea, then come back and wake her.

"Nah, fuck that, she can't be late again," he thought aloud, staring at the time. It would soon be seven. Promise walked into the bedroom and sat gently down on the bed next to her. He silently looked at his three-year old daughter, Ashley.

"Ashley, get up," he said shaking his daughter gently. "Ashley, it's time to get up for school."

Ashley didn't respond to her father's gentle nudges. She

was sound asleep.

"Ashley, c'mon, we gotta get you ready for school."

Promise threw the covers off his daughter and smiled when he saw her in her Dora the Explorer pajamas looking so cute with her hair nicely braided up and nestled against her pillow.

He picked his daughter up in his arms still trying to wake her gentle, "C'mon, baby-girl, you wanna stay up wit' daddy all night and now you can't get up in the morning. I'm gonna have to start putting you to bed earlier."

Ashley slowly opened her eyes. "Daddy, I don't wanna go to school," she said.

"Why not?"

"Because I'm tired."

Promise chuckled to himself. "You still going to school. You can take a nap later."

"Daddy, daddy I wanna sleep."

"Ahight, when you get home tonight you're going to bed early. Okay, baby girl?"

"Daddy…"

Promise picked his daughter up in his arms and carried her off to the bathroom to get her washed. He bathed his daughter at night so it was easier to get her ready in the mornings. All he had to do was use a washcloth and have her brush her teeth in the mornings.

"Ashley, brush your teeth properly now. We can't have you going to daycare with your breath stinking, okay."

Ashley stared at her father holding the toothbrush in his hand. The water was rapidly coming from the sink. This was part of their morning routine. His daughter knew what was up by now. First brush your teeth then wash your face. Then Ashley had breakfast.

Promise left her in the bathroom trusting that his daughter wouldn't give him any problems this morning. Yesterday, he went into the kitchen for ten minutes to start up breakfast. When he came back into the bathroom to check on his daughter, he found her fast asleep again on the bathroom floor. He laughed at first but had to get serious, telling her to get up and get ready for daycare.

He went into the kitchen to prepare oatmeal for his baby girl. She loved it along with Fruit Loops and candy. Promise also knew that his daughter needed to eat healthy too. He didn't want his baby girl growing up with weak bones. She was spoiled but not completely rotten.

After starting the oatmeal, he made a fresh kettle for his tea and then returned back to the bathroom to see his daughter still brushing her teeth and playing with the water. It was almost overflowing onto the floor.

"Ashley, what the hell you doing?"

"Brushin' my teeth, Daddy."

"You getting water all over the floor and look at your shirt! Damn girl! Why you always gotta make a mess?" He barked, stepping into the bathroom, shutting off the water and removing the toothbrush from her hand. "C'mon, you gotta get dressed."

He carried his daughter back into her bedroom and removed her damp pajamas tossing them to the floor. Promise shook his head peering down at her as she looked up at him, smiling. She was a mess.

"I wanna watch cartoons, Daddy. I wanna watch *Wiggles*," she said.

Wiggles was one of Ashley's favorite morning cartoons.

Watching it would certainly distract her and he didn't need that.

"Later, we gotta get you dressed for school now."

"But I wanna watch *Wiggles*, Daddy."

"Ashley, don't start today, okay?"

She started pouting, folding her arms across her chest and displaying her disagreement with her father's decision. Promise put lotion on his daughter.

"Daddy, can I please watch *Wiggles*? Please, daddy."

Promise sighed, giving into his daughter's demand. He searched for the remote to her TV, and turned to *Wiggles*. Ashley smiled, "Thank you, Daddy."

"Yeah, okay."

Promise glanced at the time. It was 7:15 a.m. He needed to be out the door by 7:45, so he'd able to reach his 8:30 appointment across town in Brooklyn. He hurried his daughter to get dressed, throwing her into her uniform, a yellow buttoned down shirt, checkered green and yellow skirt, and her cute little shoes. Then he carried his daughter into the kitchen, sat her at the table and placed a small bowl of oatmeal in front of her, telling her to eat.

"Daddy, I want honey and my juice," Ashley requested.

Rushing to the fridge and pouring his daughter a cup of red Kool Aid, Promise let out a loud sigh. He then turned on the TV in the kitchen and set the channel to *Wiggles* keeping his daughter preoccupied with her breakfast and her favorite show.

He rushed into the bedroom to get dressed. There was not enough time to shower so he washed, quickly brushing his teeth, threw on cologne and quickly put on his gray Sean John jeans, a blue Rocawear T-shirt, and beige Timberlands. Promise scurried back into kitchen to tend to his daughter.

"You finish?" he asked.

"Look daddy, I spilled my juice."

"Damn it, Ashley," Promise shouted when he saw the red Kool Aid all across the table and some on her uniform. Now he had to clean the mess and probably change her uniform.

"I'm sorry, daddy."

"Forget it. We gotta go."

Promise hurried out his fifth floor apartment in Far Rockaway, Queens. He didn't have time for the elevator. He dashed down the grungy staircase carrying his daughter in one arm and her book bag in the other. Luckily, he'd parked his X5 close by. He put Ashley in her car seat, dashed around to the driver's side, and quickly peeled away.

"Damn, I'm gonna be late," he hissed.

Promise reached the daycare at 8:15 a.m. He didn't even shut his engine off, unlocked his doors and ran around to where Ashley sat. He unbuckled her, hastily took her out of her seatbelt and rang the bell to the daycare.

"Good morning, Mr. Carter," one of the teachers at the center greeted.

"Hey, what's up? I'm in kind of a rush. Bye, Ashley. Here, give me hugs and kisses."

Ashley went to her father, giving him quick hug and kiss then turned to her daycare teacher. Promise rushed back to his jeep and sped off to Brooklyn.

It had been six months since Ashley came to live with her father. Ashley had been staying with her mother, Denise Jenkins until she was murdered. Then Ashley moved in with her father. Promise didn't mind taking on this new responsibility.

He loved his daughter to death and would do anything for her. He wasn't trying to hear about his only beloved daughter being turned over to the state, an orphan living from group home to group home, trying to be adopted like he was once. At first, it was hard for him doing what he did but they had adjusted and now he couldn't live a day without her.

Hearing about his baby mother's murder fucked him up bad. Promise couldn't sleep, eat, or do anything for two weeks. Even though they hadn't been together as a couple, they were cool. They both took good care of their daughter.

Denise was murdered by a punk-stick-up-kid, in front of her building one night in Bushwick. She had been coming home from work, getting ready to pick up her daughter from a neighbor when a young thug in a black hoodie, dark jeans and dirty black Timberlands emerged from out of nowhere startled her, demanding that she give up her purse and jewelry. He was looking jittery coming at her armed with a .357. She gave him her purse easy but was adamant about not giving up her jewelry, especially since her necklace had been a gift from her father and had been around her neck since she was six.

The young robber struggled with her for her jewelry snatching off her bracelet and when he went for her necklace, she slapped him. Denise was a tough girl from the block and seeing a gun didn't easily scare her. She was from the rough streets of Brownsville and had seen a gun before. The young thug sticking her up looked no older than sixteen and he was acting scared.

Denise was damned if some pussy-ass-broke-hood-nigga with a gun was gonna rob her of something so sentimental to her. She didn't even think that the gun was loaded. They fought and Denise was whooping his ass for a minute until the gun went off, the explosion caused her to grasp her chest. Shocked at the impact of getting shot, Denise suddenly collapsed to the ground.

That young fool snatched her diamond necklace, darted down the block and disappeared into the night leaving Denise dead. A neighbor on the first floor of Denise's building heard the gunshot and she looked out her window. She saw Denise lying face down on the concrete in front of the building with blood oozing from her gunshot wound, and immediately called the cops.

The next day, Promise heard she was murdered. He cried in front of his peeps, collapsing to the floor. Squeeze, his main nigga, tried to console him but couldn't understand the pain he felt. After all Promise wasn't living with Denise and for the most part was over her.

Within a week, Squeeze and his niggas set out for the Brooklyn streets looking for Denise's killer. They even put word on the streets that there was a $5,000 reward for any bitch or nigga willing to come forward and give information on who did it and where they were hiding. The following week, they got their results. There was a young nigga named Muddy, who was known for sticking up muthafuckas in Bushwick. He earned a deadly rep out there.

Soon after receiving the info, Squeeze and his crew caught up with Muddy. They put three shots in his head, one in the eye and two in the back of his head. They even found Denise's necklace on him—stupid muthafucka.

Promise hit the Belt Parkway doing 65 in his X5. He was on his way to Bed Stuy to meet Squeeze, Show, and Pooh, his niggas from way back when they used to wrestle each other on the playground.

Pooh was the youngest at twenty-one and he had a short temper and could be very loud and violent. He grew up in Brownsville but spent the majority of his youthful years in Bed-Stuy. To him, that was more his home than anywhere else. Pooh was 6-1, slender nigga rocking a baldy and the only nigga in the hood with hazel eyes. Bitches used to love that nigga for his eyes. He got a lot of pussy when he was young and he was still fucking.

Show, he was a big dude pushing 250 pounds. Solid muthafucka and tall too, 6-5 and looking like that nigga, Eric Sermon from EPMD. Shit, Show was always the biggest. When he was twelve, he weighed 200 pounds. They called him Show because when he used to play high school football, he used to sack the quarterback so fucking hard, it was always a show to see. People came from all corners of Brooklyn, Manhattan, and even Queens to see Show play football. It was even more of a thrill to see when he put the quarterback on his ass and tackled the breath out of his opponents on the field.

He got a scholarship to play for Virginia Tech his senior year but fucked that up. A month before his high school graduation, he was caught dealing drugs on the corner of his block.

Squeeze, was the wild and crazy nigga. He was born in Jersey and moved out to Brooklyn when he was ten. He had lived there with his moms ever since. Squeeze was twenty-five and he was the type of guy that always had to be seen and heard wherever he went. Squeeze was rowdy in the club and was always scheming.

Bitches and niggas gave him love because he was strictly

street mentality and he sported a don't-give-a-fuck-about-life attitude. A nigga fucked with Squeeze, a nigga better come correct or don't come at all because Squeeze didn't forget shit. He didn't forgive easily and held grudges. Squeeze was not a big dude, 5'9, 157 pounds with gentle features and a little bit of well-groomed facial hair. He was a slim nigga with short hair but was real gangsta.

Then there was Promise, the fourth member. He hooked up with Squeeze, Show, and Pooh when he was thirteen after he moved to Brooklyn from Queens. It took him a while to fit in but he eventually did and the four guys had been like brothers since. They mostly hung out over on Fulton and Throop. Promise always had a nonchalant attitude being a cool ass nigga. He got lots of respect from niggas for being Squeeze's boy and he looked out for many niggas back in the day when they got into trouble.

Promise put in his Ashante CD and cruised into Brooklyn. Under the driver's seat, was a loaded silver .32 which had never been used. He just kept it under his seat for protection. No bodies, no nothing. Promise had kept the gun closer for a year now.

For some reason when he hit Atlantic Blvd, Promise started thinking about his life and the man he had become. He didn't hold a nine to five like most average folks. He didn't run the streets on a daily basis like his nigga, Squeeze, and the others. Promise didn't fuck around with many women like he used to do back in the days. Ever since he got custody of his daughter, the flow of pussy had slowed. He spent more time with his daughter, and loving every minute of it.

Promise tried to live a normal life but that was difficult when raising a child and at the same time being a Brooklyn stick-up kid. It was how he made his money. Promise was robbing niggas in the hood, pimps, hustlers, and drug dealers. Shit, if they were balling and flashing then they would just get got.

Squeeze played the game like that and brought the others in. He was always plotting and scheming, finally he put his niggas on.

"We can make some real money," he had told them. "Real money, real soon," Squeeze had said.

Lately Promise had been feeling a change of heart about what he did. He had Ashley to take care of and didn't wanna take a chance of losing his daughter by getting got out there or, getting locked up, worse, being killed by robbing one of the wrong niggas in the streets. He'd been having a change of heart lately wanting out but the money was too good.

Squeeze and the team had been doing what they do for years now. They had their ups and downs in the game but on the real, shit paid off for niggas. They were all pushing nice cars and flossing nice jewelry and clothes. In one month, niggas might make up to $25,000, maybe $30,000 if shit flowed right for them and that's if they caught a true baller lapsing.

They might catch that nigga for a few bricks and then they'd go out to Jersey and hustle them same keys for a wholesale price, hooking niggas up out there lovely. And if it came down to it, they might occasionally go out and do some B & E's, hitting up homes in Long Island, Staten Island, and even New Jersey. Squeeze got his niggas into all kinds of shit because he was a money nigga, a hustler willing and ready to get that money by any means necessary.

The one good thing about Promise's track record in his life of crime was that he had never killed anyone. Too bad he couldn't speak for the rest of the fellows in his crew especially Squeeze. Promise might have been an accessory to murder, assault, and other shit like that but the nigga never took a life, never pulled the trigger therefore, the nigga can sometimes sleep easy at nights. Lately, even being an accomplice still fucked with his conscience.

He planned to meet with Squeeze and the rest of the guys around 8:30 at Squeeze's uncle's crib. Squeeze's uncle was an ol' school hustler who'd been in and out of prison since he was fifteen. He stayed in the basement with his girl in a brownstone on Kingston Ave. His girl's family had the rest of the crib upstairs.

Promise was late pulling up in front of the place at 9:15. He rushed out his vehicle and dashed down the steps, ringing the basement bell. Squeeze's Uncle Junior answered the door in dirty jeans and a torn wife-beater.

"Nigga, you late," Uncle Junior stated with a cigarette dangling from his lips. "You got my nephew waiting for your punk ass. We got work to do, nigga!"

Promise looked at Uncle Junior not even acknowledging his presence and walked right by him. Promise entered the basement apartment and saw his niggas sitting on an old green couch smoking trees and talking.

"Damn, Promise. What da fuck, yo? You got us waiting down here forever," Pooh shouted.

"Nigga, I had to take my daughter to school, ahight?" Promise answered with annoyance.

"Yeah, whatever, my nigga," Squeeze said getting up out of his seat and approaching Promise. He gave him dap and a hug. "I'm glad you came anyway. You know we can't do this shit without you, my nigga."

"I still say you should leave his punk ass out and bring me in wit' y'all. I need to get dis money too, nigga," Uncle Junior chimed in, swaggering into the room behind Promise. His breath was reeking of alcohol.

"Uncle Junior, look at you. It ain't even noon yet and you're halfway drunk, man. Nigga, you stay your ass home. Niggas can't be having you fuck our shit up."

Uncle Junior plopped down on the couch next to Show. Show never liking the nigga, glared at him. Uncle Junior was not a well-liked guy in da hood. He was considered a fuck up to most and a drunk to many. It was a wonder how his woman put up with him. He wasn't about shit and never would be.

It was even a shock that the nigga got a bitch to have under his arms at all. Carina, they say she was too nice of a girl to be with a man like Uncle Junior. She was a pretty bitch too. The nigga must've got that magic-stick to keep a woman like her around.

"Uncle Junior, your breath stinks!" Show insulted rising out of his seat and sitting down next to Pooh.

"Fuck y'all niggas. Y'all mutha-fuckas gonna give me respect in my own damn house," Junior demanded.

"Fuck you, drunk," Show replied. "I wanna see you throw me out."

"Youngblood, don't fuckin' test me. I don't give a fuck how drunk you may think I am or how big your fat ass is. I'll still..."

"Y'all two just shut da fuck up for now. Dammit! Y'all

niggas acting like bitches," Squeeze shouted.

"Call your fuckin' uncle off then, Squeeze," Show said.

"Show, chill out. We got business to take care of today. You wanna get this money today? Huh, nigga?"

"Ahigit, Uncle Junior take your ass in the back room so me and my niggas can talk some business."

"Why, it's my place, nigga! I don't see you paying rent here," Junior exclaimed.

"Nigga, I said take your fuckin' ass into the back room before I come over there and get real on you," Squeeze shouted.

Uncle Junior appeared punk'd, getting screamed on by his own flesh and blood, slowly stood up. He peered around and slowly walked off to the bedroom in the back. Everyone waited and watched, making sure he was gone before getting back to the business at hand.

"I got word on them niggas that be over on Tompkins and Myrtle. They holding serious weight up in them buildings," Squeeze informed his niggas. "I've been staking the place out regularly."

"So what you saying, Squeeze? You ready to hit 'em up?" Pooh asked.

"Yeah."

"When?"

"Today."

"Nigga is you crazy!" Promise interjected, "We ain't plan for dis shit. We don't know what those niggas are holding up in there and how many niggas be up in there. It's too risky, Squeeze."

"Fuck dat! They ain't packin' heat like that. Niggas up in them buildings are too laidback. They be thinking niggas can't get at them. They thinking they can't get got, Promise. We gotta let 'em know."

"Fuck it, nigga. I'm down for it," Show said.

"What about you, Pooh? The money's there, no question to it. If we don't get at these niggas today, no telling when might be our next chance."

"Fuck it! I'm in too," Pooh agreed.

Squeeze looked over at Promise who was still standing, "Promise, we need you, baby. You know we can't do dis shit without you, nigga. We a team. We get dat money together or we don't get dat money at all."

Promise sighed. "Ahight, yo, I'm in."

"My nigga."

"You got a plan for dis shit, Squeeze cause I ain't trying to fuck up getting this money," Show said putting the cigarette to his lips and taking a quick drag.

"Of course, nigga. I wouldn't have brought the shit up if I didn't."

"How we gonna do this?" Pooh questioned.

"Like I said, them niggas up in the Tompkins housing are too laid-back wit' their shit. They slipping, baby. Majority of them niggas that be up in there running business in them apartments are young niggas and they pussy. So we ain't got nuthin' to worry about."

"But who backing them?" Promise asked.

"Some new nigga from Jersey. He go by the name Nine. And he workin' wit' his cousin from Flatbush. He got shit stashed in his cousin's crib. I say about three or four keys of weed and about half a key of dat powder. They moving shit in and out of the apartment like crazy. Money's coming in, and lots of it. We ain't gotta worry about Nine. It's his cousin we gotta worry about. He got clout but da nigga's outta town 'til Thursday so we gotta move early. I got this girl that be up in the buildings. She be giving me the rundown when they be moving and where they be moving they shit. If we hit 'em up today, we hittin' the jackpot."

"But why hit 'em in daylight?" Promise asked.

"It's too risky during the night. Niggas be runnin' around at that time. Plus, dats when they expect jackas to come. They more alert during the night. We gotta hit 'em early today. They ain't gonna be expecting niggas like us to be comin' through durin' broad daylight. I've passed there a few times durin' the day and it be off da hook up in dat bitch. Them young niggas be sitting around playing Game Boy, chattin' on their cellie, serving customers, and pullin' bread. They don't be on point like that. We do it right and we got this money in da bag."

"I feel you, Squeeze," Pooh replied taking a pull from the weed.

Promise glanced at the time and it was 10:00. He had to pick his daughter up from daycare around five. He prayed that this job would go right. His daughter needed him after school and he couldn't afford to lose his baby girl over some bullshit.

"This shit better work, Squeeze. I got my little girl to go home to."

"Trust a nigga, Promise. Damn, how many years have we been out here doing this shit, catching niggas slipping and we didn't fuck up yet? I know what da fuck I'm doing. I ain't no rookie nigga out here tryi..g to get my dick wet in the game. My shit always comes through," Squeeze said oozing with confidence.

Around noon, all four hopped into Squeeze's truck, a burgundy GMC, and headed down Bedford Ave toward the Tompkins Houses to pull off their heist. Squeeze drove, Show rode shotgun, and Promise and Pooh occupied the backseat. They all were heavily armed. Promise had a .380 and Pooh was always armed with a silver 9mm. Squeeze and Show both had .45s and were ready to use deadly force if it became necessary.

They reached Tompkins in a short time. Everyone knew their job and was savvy on how to put it in effect. Squeeze stepped outta the truck first. He was parked three blocks away and walked down Tompkins with Show by his side.

The target was on the 8th floor, a two-bedroom apartment. Squeeze knew how these young niggas operated their business. It was definitely sloppy and he wondered why these niggas ain't get got for their shit yet.

Squeeze approached one of the young hustler's on the street while he was sitting on a milk crate, talking to some bitch on his phone. He didn't even notice Squeeze coming until he was up on him.

"Yo, son, you got dat trees?" Squeeze asked.

The young hustler looked up and Squeeze didn't look like a threat, just looked like some average nigga wanting to get high. Of course the young nigga didn't know his rep.

"What you want? Choc lit' or haze?" the young kid asked.

"I'm looking for ounces. Nine sent me through. Told me y'all lil' niggas can hook a nigga up wid da bomb-shit."

The young kid stared at Squeeze with quick doubtful eyes. "You know Nine?" he asked.

"Yeah, I'm here from Jersey City."

"Oh word? You from Jersey, huh?"

"Yeah..."

"Ahight, upstairs, son. Got my nigga, Shawn, holding

down business on the 8th floor. It's going for 12 large. You feel me?"

Squeeze reached into his pocket and pulled out a wad of hundreds. The young hustler's eyes lit up when he saw all that money.

"How many niggas up there?" Squeeze asked, looking like he was paranoid in front of dude.

"You scared, son? We ain't gonna take your money...you know Nine...anyway, my nigga Shawn and D up there. They good. Knock at apartment 8D. Three slow knocks will get you in."

Squeeze smiled, thinking to himself that this was a dumb nigga; these muthafuckas definitely deserved to get got for their shit. First off, the nigga talked too fuckin' much and second, the nigga was too trusting and those were two fatal mistakes.

Show was standing by the corner and Pooh and Promise were already in the building waiting to move. Shit was too easy. They didn't even need a four-man crew to pull it off.

"Good lookin' out, yo," Squeeze thanked, stepping back from da nigga.

Squeeze thought to himself that after they were done handling their business upstairs, robbing these clown ass niggas in the apartment, he was going to come back down and handle son sitting on the milk crate, get him for everything he got. The young hustler went back to chatting with some bitch on his cellphone. He walked into the building lobby where Promise and Pooh were waiting. Show stepped in a few seconds later.

"What I tell y'all niggas, easy money to get got. C'mon, let's get this shit over wid. I got some pussy to tend to later," Squeeze announced.

They all walked into the elevator and rode it to the 8th floor.

Squeeze and Pooh stepped out first; their guns concealed in their waistbands. They looked for the apartment and Squeeze felt so sorry for these dumb niggas he almost let out a laugh.

"8D, here we go," Squeeze said.

Promise and Show were standing guard by the elevator. Squeeze didn't want too many niggas by the door. He didn't want to intimidate da niggas inside. Squeeze gave the apartment door three slow knocks like money downstairs told him to do. A few seconds later, he heard locks being unlocked and the door opened. A young baby faced nigga answered. He had his shirt off exposing his bird looking chest.

"You Shawn?" Squeeze asked.

"Yeah, Donny sent y'all niggas up?" He asked.

"We lookin' to get some onions."

"Ahight." Shawn peered at Pooh for a minute. The tall slim nigga invited the two in and shut the door behind them.

Squeeze cased the joint quickly. Glancing around looking for the second guy and trying to see how many rooms there were. The apartment was sparsely furnished with a run down looking couch, a few chairs and tables set up, no carpeting, the smell of weed lingering in the air. Yeah, Squeeze was definitely in the right apartment.

"Yo, I'm gonna have to search the two of y'all," Shawn said to them.

Squeeze and Pooh let out a slight smirk.

"Whatever, yo," Pooh replied.

Shawn went up to Pooh and started to pat him down but before he could reach around his waist and the feel the gun that Pooh was concealing, Squeeze swiftly pulled out his .45 and quickly put it to Shawn's temple.

"Shut da fuck up and don't move, nigga, before I blow your fuckin' head off," Squeeze warned.

"Yo, chill, chill, chill, yo," Shawn stuttered in a panicky voice. He had his arms raised and Squeeze forced him down on his knees.

"Where your boy at?" Squeeze asked.

"Huh?"

"Nigga, don't play dumb. Where da fuck is your boy?" Squeeze asked again pressing the tip of the .45 harder against Shawn's skull. He didn't want to alert the second man or whoever was in the house.

"I think he's in da bathroom."

Squeeze nodded his head toward Pooh and Pooh quickly went toward the bathroom. The bathroom door was shut and locked indicating someone was in there. Pooh stood flushed by the wall outside the bathroom door waiting. They heard the toilet flush and the sink running. Then the bathroom door opened up and another slender young male stepped out wearing a white T and blue jeans but before he even took three steps, Pooh lunged at duke jerking him by the arm and placing the barrel of the .45 to his skull. The young stranger suddenly began to panic, having a .45 pressed to his head.

"Don't kill me, please...I ain't carrying, yo...believe me," the young stranger said to the two young men.

"Y'all get on your knees, now!" Squeeze ordered.

The two men did as told and rested down on their knees with their fingers locked behind their heads and peered up at Pooh and Squeeze who had them at gunpoint.

"Where da shit?" Squeeze asked.

Neither answered. They both glanced at each other.

"Oh, no one heard me?" Squeeze angrily uttered and to let niggas know he was serious, Squeeze suddenly started to pistol whip one of the two men striking him multiple times against his face wit' the .45. Shawn bellowed. His friend did nothing but watch.

"Ahight yo, I'm gonna ask again and if I don't hear shit, dats my word. One a y'all niggas is dying in here today," Squeeze said cocking back his gat. "Where da shit at?"

"It's in the bathroom, the two cabinets under the sink," the second dude answered softly.

"You sure?"

He nodded his head in affirmation.

"Pooh, go get dat."

Pooh scurried into the bathroom while Squeeze kept them at gunpoint. Promise and Show remained outside the apartment keeping watch by the elevator. Promise was wondering what was taking these two niggas so long. He couldn't help but glance at his watch every passing minute. While inside, Pooh came back out with two big black garbage bags filled with weed and coke, good shit.

"Bingo," he uttered. Squeeze smiled.

"Y'all some dumb ass niggas. You know how easy this shit was to get. Thank y'all. We need dumb mu'fuckas like y'all so me and my niggas can continue to get our money easy," Squeeze said.

"What we gonna do with 'em?" Pooh asked.

"How old are y'all?" Squeeze asked.

"Eighteen," Shawn muttered out with his mouth filled with blood, his jaw swollen.

"And you, nigga?"

"Seventeen."

"Listen here, today, I'm gonna let y'all two niggas live. But if I ever hear my name come out y'all mouths about me robbing y'all, I swear, I'm gonna come back for y'all two and murder y'all. Don't ever fuckin' sleep on Squeeze, ya heard me?"

They both nodded.

"Tell dat nigga, Nine, I said what's up."

"But you said don't speak your name," Shawn said.

"Oh, yeah...dats right...you on point now, son...stay dat way from now on. Yo, Pooh, lets be out."

Squeeze and Pooh dashed outta 8D and met up with Show and Promise. "We good, niggas." They all got back into the elevator.

Down in the lobby as all four men exited the elevator, they saw Donny entering the lobby. Squeeze couldn't help but to let out a broad smile, uttering to his niggas, "Yo, dis shit is too fuckin' easy...I'm about to cum on myself."

They snatched up Donny, beat the shit outta him in the staircase, snatched his jewelry and money then took his sneakers for the fun of it. They arrived at Junior's a half-hour later and counted up their take. The haul netted $7,000 cash, mad pounds of weed and cocaine to sell. The jooks came off damn good.

Cash was divided, $1,750 each, and plans were made to hustle the weed off into the streets. Squeeze didn't give a fuck about retaliation or repercussions. He felt that Nine and his crew were too soft for them niggas to come back on some gangsta shit.

Promise took his cut of the money, jumped back into his X5, and headed back to Queens. Another day, another dollar.

5:00 p.m. Monday through Friday, Promise was at the daycare faithfully to pick up his daughter, Ashley.

"Daddy, daddy!" Ashley shouted out excited about seeing her father every evening when he came by to scoop up his lil' girl. She jumped into his arms and it was routine everyday that he gave his daughter a hug and kiss.

"You miss me?"

Ashley nodded yes.

"Go get your stuff. We gotta go."

She jumped out of her father's arms and went to retrieve her book bag and other belongings.

"Hey, Mr. Carter," Ms. Ways said.

"Hey, how was she today?" he asked.

"She was good but she didn't take her nap today and she didn't eat much lunch. But she's a good child, very attentive in class, gets along with the other children. She's a sweetheart," Ms. Ways informed Promise.

"That's my little girl." Promise shook his head.

"Daddy...Daddy, look what I drew in school today," Ashley shouted out showing her father a picture of some animals.

"Oh, that's pretty. You ready?"

Ashley nodded her head.

"Okay."

"Bye, Miss Way," Ashley said to her teacher.

"Bye, Ashley. See you tomorrow. You have a nice night, Mr. Carter."

"You too," he replied and walked out the door with his daughter.

"Daddy, I want McDonalds," Ashley whined.

Promise sighed, shaking his head. "Ahight, we'll eat McDonalds today."

After their small lunch together, Promise returned home and had his daughter do her homework right away, tracing letters and numbers and coloring some objects. Later he prepared her dinner, spaghetti and meatballs, one of her favorites. They watched TV together and Ashley fell asleep in her daddy's arms.

Later, Promise picked his daughter up and carried her inside the bedroom. He prepared her for bed, putting on her pajamas while she groggily complied. He covered her gently, and said a short prayer. Soon as he stepped out her bedroom, his cellphone went off.

"Yeah, who this?"

"Squeeze, nigga. You good tonight?"

"Nah, my daughter's sleep."

"Damn! I got a job for us," Squeeze said.

"Nigga…you gonna have to do without me."

"Big money in dis, nigga. You can't get one of those bitches in your building to baby sit?" he asked, sounding annoyed.

"I'm a fall back tonight. You got Pooh and Show. They can do work."

"But I need my right-hand-man."

"Sorry Squeeze. I'm a have to take a rain check on this one."

"Damn! Ahight, hit me up tomorrow. One, my nigga."

"One," Promise replied, clicking off, and plopping his behind down on the couch, a little stressed.

Taking care of his daughter 24/7 and doing what he did out there on the streets was definitely taking a toll on him. He massaged his forehead with his fingertips, squinted his eyes, and thought about shit. He missed his daughter's mother so much.

She made shit simple on him when she was still alive but now that she was gone, the burden of weight was passed to him and it was stressing him the fuck out. He wanted to live a normal life. He wanted to get the fuck away from the street but making that easy money while dealing with Squeeze was tempting, easy, and profitable.

And besides, Promise thought, even if he did want to become legit and stay outta the life of crime and get himself a legit job, he had a criminal record and his background was tarnished from past mistakes. Yet, every night after placing his daughter down to sleep, he asked himself how long could this life style last?

Everything comes to an end. He couldn't risk losing his daughter because she was all he had that was important in the world. He wanted to see her grow to be in her life constantly. He wanted a way out and kept pondering on how. Promise ended up falling asleep on the couch dozing off while watching the news.

Next morning they were running on time. He got Ashley up and ready for school early and was at the daycare at ten minutes to eight. Promise got out his Jeep a bit more cheerful today. He unbuckled his daughter from the car seat and allowed her to run up to the door and knock twice, indicating her presence.

The school door slowly opened up and Ashley ran inside with Promise right behind carrying her book-bag. When he stepped in, he was stunned and completely taken back by a beautiful young female standing in front of him.

"Good morning," she softly announced smiling and peering down at Ashley. She bent over and rested her hands on her knees.

"Hi," Ashley shyly responded with her soft voice, peering back at the beautiful young woman who was a stranger.

"And what's your name?" the young lady asked.

"Ashley," she slowly announced her name.

"Hi, Ashley. My name is Audrey."

"Hi, Audrey."

Audrey looked back at Promise, smiled and admired the handsome young man standing behind who she assumed to be Ashley's father.

"Hello," she politely introduced herself to Promise, extending her hand. Promise couldn't help but stare. She was gorgeous. Exquisite. He knew it was impolite to stare the way he was but he couldn't help himself. His eyes were transfixed.

"You must be her father?"

"Um…yes…she's my girl."

"She's so cute. Oh, I'm Audrey," she said extending her right hand.

"Hey, how you doing, Audrey," he responded holding her hand a moment too long. "I'm Promise," he said blushing slightly which was something Promise rarely did.

"Promise," she smiled, "that's a unique name."

"I'm a unique person," he flirted.

She smiled. Audrey's golden brown complexion and deep brown eyes caught the eyes of many men. She had long silky hair, full luscious lips, and an hourglass figure with breasts so big they looked like balloons ready to pop. Promise glimpsed her breasts and smiled more widely. Enticing, Audrey definitely was.

"Um, what happened to Ms. Ways?" Promise asked.

"Oh, she called in sick this morning and today's my first day."

"Oh, welcome."

"Thank you. I'm a little nervous," she proclaimed.

"Oh, don't be...you seem cool. I know you'll get along good wit' the children. I see my daughter already likes you."

"You think?"

"I can tell."

Audrey smiled. She liked Promise and felt attracted to him. He seemed cool enough. She gave him respect and liked that he was taking care of his daughter and bringing her into daycare every morning.

One of the other staff interrupted their conversation and called out to Audrey. "Oh, um...it was nice meeting you, Promise."

"Same here," he replied. He glanced around for his daughter and called out for her. "Give daddy a hug and kiss before I leave." Ashley ran into her father's arm and gave him a quick hug and kiss on his cheek.

"Bye, baby."

"Bye, Daddy."

Audrey smiled, loving the sight. "Daddy's little girl," she uttered to Promise.

He smiled and causally exited. When he was outside,

he shouted, "Damn, she fine." He smiled so hard that he almost caught lockjaw.

Promise made his way back into Brooklyn to get up with Squeeze and the rest of his niggas. During the entire drive, he was obsessed by thoughts about Audrey. He wondered if she had a man or worse, was she married? Nah, there was no wedding ring on her finger. He was hoping that she was single.

When he got to Bed-Stuy, he parked his X5 and went into a nearby McDonalds for a quick hash brown and sausage, egg, and biscuit meal. Half-hour later, he met up with Squeeze and Show over at Uncle Junior's crib again.

When he stepped in, they were doing nothing but lounging around in the basement and getting high off the marijuana they'd lifted yesterday.

"Where Pooh at?" Promise asked.

Squeeze shrugged his shoulders. "Don't know."

"Damn nigga, why you grinning so hard?" Show asked.

"Nigga musta gotten some good pussy," Squeeze said then took a pull from da weed.

"Nah, I'm just in a good mood."

"Nigga, you got some pussy. Don't front. Shit musta been some real good pussy cuz you got da ill Kool Aid smile."

Promise didn't respond to Squeeze's remark. He was on a natural high. He couldn't get Audrey off his mind. They'd just met but there was something about her he liked. They clicked this morning.

"You wanna hit this?" Squeeze asked passing Promise dat choc lit.

"Nah, I'm good."

"You sure, nigga?"

Promise nodded.

"Should I have to remind you young blood that it's puff-puff-pass da shit," Uncle Junior intervened reaching for the weed.

Squeeze glared over at his uncle. They were family by blood but didn't get along. They were cool at some points but hated each other. Uncle Junior despised his nephew because when he saw him, he saw something he should've been, could've been.

When Squeeze looked over at his uncle, he saw nothing but a fuck-up, a disgrace to the family name. Uncle Junior wasn't shit but a leach, living off bitches and begging for dollars. And the nigga was only forty-five years old.

"Uncle Junior you ain't put in for dis here," Squeeze said to him passing him the blunt and doing him a favor, "so don't ask me no more."

"Ahight, young blood, whatever! We still fam."

"Yeah, whatever, nigga. I gotta go take a piss," Squeeze said rising and heading into the bathroom. "Show, hold dat down."

Show nodded. Promise took a seat opposite Show, picked up a Don Diva magazine and started flipping through the pages.

"So, what y'all niggas getting into today?" Promise asked.

Show shrugged his shoulder and uttered, "Don't know... chillin' right now."

Promise glanced around the room real quick. He saw Show getting high and slouching down in the couch. He looked over at Uncle Junior who looked to be in his own little world, still in that same wife-beater, torn jeans, and lips looking black as ever. Uncle Junior seemed to be lost in contemplation, just staring at the wall.

Promise was getting tired of doing the same old shit wit' the same old niggas. He shook his head as he looked around the room and thought how many countless hours he had spent down in this basement getting high with these niggas, scheming with Squeeze, counting stolen money and waiting for bitches to come through. Everyday he'd drop his daughter off and bring his black ass back into Brooklyn knowing it was hot for him out here.

Everyone was in the basement when a loud knock came from the front door.

"Yo, Junior, get dat. It's probably Pooh," Show said.

"Man, do I look like your bitch to you," Uncle Junior replied back. "Get da door your fuckin' self."

"What nigga?"

"Y'all niggas chill. I'll get da fuckin' door," Promise said getting out his seat and walking to the door.

"Who…?"

"Pooh, nigga, open da fuck up."

Promise began to unlock the door and Pooh came flying into the crib, almost collapsing over Promise.

"What da fuck!" Promise cursed but saw Pooh, bloodied face, swollen eye and his gear in shreds. Promise became concerned. "What happened to you?"

"Niggas jumped me."

"What?"

By this time, Squeeze was out the bathroom and when he saw Pooh all fucked up, he shouted, "Pooh, who da fuck did dat to you?"

"Niggas we got at yesterday. They came back and caught me alone over on Myrtle."

"What? Don't worry 'bout dat shit, Pooh. We gonna handle it for you," Squeeze said, getting excited. "Dem pussy niggas came back at you...how da fuck did they know where you were at?"

"Nine... He was with 'em niggas too."

Squeeze had no more words. He was ready to take action. He got his gat and cocked it. Show and Pooh were ready to peel off at the niggas who had disrespected the team. Promise lingered behind. He wanted no parts of any street beef.

"Promise, you coming?" Squeeze asked seeing his nigga not making an effort to follow him into his truck to get revenge.

"We don't even know where these niggas be at," Promise said.

"I know where," Pooh countered.

"C'mon nigga, fuck you acting like you pussy for? Niggas jumped Pooh. He family, don't front on us Promise. Word, my nigga."

Clearly apprehensive, Promise took a deep breath. He knew how Squeeze and the rest got down when they felt disrespected and truth be told, he didn't want any part of that. His daughter loomed in his mind and he prayed shit didn't hit the fan right now. Promise followed Squeeze and the rest. They all piled into Squeeze's Dinali and sped down Throop Avenue. All were packing. Promise sat in the back while Pooh rode shotgun. Pooh's silver nine millimeter sat on his lap, and Squeeze's .380, was next to him.

When they got over by the Tompkins Housing area, they were in luck. Them same lame ass wanna be hustling niggas were still loitering out in front of the building and Nine was there with them this time.

"Fuck dat!" Squeeze shouted.

He busted a quick U-turn, sped down the block, and came to a complete stop. He caught everyone's attention. All four came jumping out wit' their guns blazing, firing at their targets. Nine and his niggas took quick cover while pulling out their guns to shoot back. Multiple gunshots rang out. Uninvolved bystanders took cover wherever they felt safe, ducking behind trees, squatting down next to cars, or running into lobbies. It was early afternoon and niggas were shooting up the neighborhood like it was the Middle East.

Promise fired but wasn't trying to hit anyone. He was just firing to be firing. He also took cover behind Squeeze's Yukon and heard bullets whizzing by his ear. His heart pounded rapidly and it felt like it was about to explode out of his chest. He wanted out of this shit and this crazy fucking world that he was in.

Squeeze and his niggas quickly jumped back into the truck when they heard sirens and sped off. Nine and his niggas also took off. All that shooting, and no one had gotten hit.

"Take me back to my fuckin' car!" Promise demanded.

"Nigga, you ahight?" Show asked.

"Just take me back to my fuckin' ride," Promise reiterated.

No one said a word. Squeeze just drove Promise back to his ride and when he got out, they quickly pulled off not uttering a word. Promise jumped into his ride and started the ignition.

He sat for a while with the Jeep in park and thanked God he was okay. Shit could've gotten a lot worse. His heartbeat was coming so fast like he was about to have an anxiety attack. He hadn't been in a shootout and it was scary, a fucked up situation to be in. Promise had busted his gun before but having niggas busting back was a whole new ballgame.

When he got his nerves together, he put his X5 in drive and drove back to Queens, back to his place where he needed to chill out for a minute and be alone.

At 5:00 p.m. that same afternoon, Promise left to pick up his daughter. He couldn't help but think that he could've died earlier, caught a stray bullet or worse been locked up. And then where would his daughter be? Probably snatched up and placed in an orphanage. He started crying while he drove.

When he reached the daycare, Promise pulled up in front and sat for a moment. He dried his eyes with the sleeve of his shirt, took in a deep breath and exited. Promise knocked on the door and Audrey answered.

"Hey, you," she kindly greeted looking excited to see him once again. "Ashley," she turned her head and called out, "your daddy's here."

Ashley jumped up outta her chair and ran to her daddy shouting, "Daddy," and jumped into his arms.

"Go get your stuff, baby girl," Promise said not looking too enthusiastic.

"You okay?" Audrey asked looking concerned.

"Yeah, I'm good…just had a rough day," he explained.

"I understand. We all have one sometime. Try not to stress it…tomorrow will be better," she said smiling.

Promise looked into her deep hypnotic brown eyes and

returned her smile. He knew her for one day and already she had made him feel good. He just wanted to grasp her in his arms and become lost in her bliss. She was all-woman and she was the kind of woman he needed in his life. She reminded him of Ashley's mother.

Ashley came over to her father with her things in her arms. He threw on her book bag and began to head for the door.

"Bye, Ashley," Audrey said.

"Bye, Miss Audrey," Ashley said back waving bye.

"Bye, you," she said to Promise smiling at him.

Promise smiled back. "Bye, see you tomorrow."

Audrey continued to smile as she watched Promise exit with his daughter. "Cute," she uttered to herself and then went back to attend to the other children left in the room.

A few days passed and Promise contemplated asking Audrey out. Not a date or nothing, he just wanted to chill. He loved her company even though so far it had only been for short periods of times when dropping off and picking his daughter up from daycare. He thought about her constantly.

He tried to chill from hanging out in Brooklyn too much, especially wit' his niggas but when Squeeze called him up to talk about making that money, he was down for it. He needed to keep bringing in that paper so he and his daughter could live.

The other day, they committed a string of B & E's out in Long Island and the other night, they fucked up a pimp over by Pennsylvania Ave and raped his hoe. Promise stood on the sideline watching while Squeeze, Show and Pooh each did they thang wit' the trick running up in her raw too.

Promise felt that shit was getting too hot in Brooklyn and Squeeze was wilding the fuck out. He was out of control. For Squeeze, it wasn't even about the money anymore. It was about the thrill, the love of being out there on the streets and terrorizing, dominating, or causing as much chaos as he could. Squeeze was about making his paper but the nigga was also about maintaining his rep. He was wild, crazy, and fearless and the beef escalating between Nine and Squeeze wasn't making the streets in Brooklyn any safer for him.

Thursday evening, Promise ran late when it came time to pick up his daughter. While driving, he glanced at the time on the radio and it was close. He got caught up and the daycare closed at 6:30 pm. If the parent was running late, the staff would drop the child off at a nearby day care and they'd keep the child till eight. But the parent is charged an extra $20 for every night he or she picks the child later.

Promise's X5 came to a screeching stop on the sidewalk and he dashed out his Jeep and ran toward the building.

"Shit," he mumbled.

He knocked on the door and felt relieved when Audrey answered.

"There you are. We started to become worried," Audrey

said smiling as usual. "Ashley, your daddy's finally here."

"Daddy," Ashley excitedly shouted out. As usual, she came running into her daddy's arms.

"Get your stuff, baby girl."

"You had us worried there for a minute," Audrey said to him.

"I lost track of time. I'm sorry."

"That's okay. It's understandable. Things happen."

There was a brief pause as they waited for Ashley. Promise wanted to ask her out but felt hesitant. Do it, ask her out, he told himself. He peered at her. She was still close to him and was attending to the other three children still left waiting. He wasn't shy when it came to the ladies but there was just something about her that made him kinda nervous. Maybe it was the fact that he actually liked her and wanted to spend time with her instead of trying to fuck her.

"Um…Audrey, can I talk to you for a minute?" he asked.

Ashley came up to her father saying, "I'm ready, daddy."

"Give me a minute, sweetheart. Watch television and give Daddy a minute."

Audrey came closer to him. The aura and her perfume enticed him and become embedded into Promise's mind. He felt hypnotized.

"This kinda hard for me," he admitted.

She raised her eyebrow at him curious as to what he had to say. "What is it?" she asked.

He let out a quick sigh and then just bluntly came out with it. "Are you busy sometime tomorrow night?"

She smiled. "Why, Promise, are you asking me out on a date?"

"Nah, nah…it ain't nuthin' like dat. I'm just sayin' you seem to be cool peoples and I wouldn't mind chillin' wit' you a little more often. You know, besides seeing you twice a day for my daughter. I mean, if dats ahight wit' you?"

She let out a slight giggle and stared into his eyes. Audrey definitely was attracted to him, no doubt. She loved his style and, to be honest, she liked and admired the street in him. Audrey knew he was from the hood by the way he come bopping in there for his daughter with baggy designer jeans, fresh new Timberlands on his feet, freestyle braids in his hair, and the trendy, hood-rich chain around his neck. Audrey thought he was cool and the fact that he loved his daughter so much and took care of her on a daily basis gave him extra points.

"You say tomorrow night?" she asked.

"I know a cool spot for us to chill out, dance and maybe have a few drinks."

"Oh, that sounds cool. I like that."

"But you sure it's okay, you won't get into trouble for dating a parent, right?"

She laughed. "Nah, I'm sure the folks in here won't have a beef with that. I'm old enough."

Promise smiled. "Ahight."

"Oh, I forgot."

"What? What happened?" Promise asked becoming suddenly worried. "You don't have a man?"

"No, tomorrow night, I promised to hang with my home girl. It's her birthday this weekend and we were supposed to do our thing together."

"Oh, she can hang. I don't mind."

"Maybe you can bring a friend with you so she won't feel

awkward," Audrey suggested.

"She ain't ugly?" he asked.

Audrey chuckled, "Nah, she's cute. I'll vouch for her."

"Ahight, I'm gonna take your word for it. I got someone in mind that'll probably come along."

"Okay so tomorrow night. It's a date."

"Say around eight."

"That's perfect," she assured him.

They both smiled and Promise called to his daughter. He hadn't felt this good and been in this kind of mood in a long time. He felt like jumping up and down and doing cartwheels. The nigga was ecstatic about tomorrow night.

Friday evening came and Promise was ready to roll. He dropped Ashley off with his neighbor, Ms. Watts. She was like family, very charming, and very motherly to Promise and his daughter. She constantly baked and cooked for the two and loved watching Ashley whenever Promise dropped her by. It was a second home to her. Ms. Watts was dependable.

Promise met Squeeze at Nelson's Barbershop, a popular neighborhood hangout in East Flatbush Avenue. He parked the X5 and walked into the crowded barbershop.

"What's poppin?" Promise greeted Tech outside.

"I got that Jigga remix with Kanye West and Lil' Wayne. I know you gon' feel it, one hundred," Tech offered returning the pound.

"Got dat old-school R&B shit?"

"You know I do. I got some classic Jodeci, 112, player," Tech said shoving couple CD's in Promise's hand.

"Now you talking," Promise chuckled.

He handed Tech ten bucks and walked into the barbershop. Squeeze was already in a chair, getting done up.

"What up?" Promise greeted Nelson, the owner and gave Squeeze a pound.

"You next," Nelson said. "Rick got your spot reserved."

"Good-looking out, Nel," Promise said and gave Rick dap as he sat in the chair.

"How you like it?"

"Just line me up," Promise said glancing at himself in the mirror.

"No doubt," Rick said.

Promise sat in Rick's chair as Nelson continued giving Squeeze a fresh one. Othe patrons spend time watching videos playing on BET. Heads of customers and barbers alike swiveled to check Jigga's latest video.

"I done told y'all them chicks don't make a dime, shaking ass in those videos, you feeling me on that?" Nelson announced.

"C'mon Nel, you know they eating. I used to date one of 'em video-hos, I mean chick and I'm sayin', the bitch was getting paid," Rick said smiling.

"Would you let your daughter become a video ho?" Nelson asked.

"My daughter…? My daughter's gonna be a lawyer or a doctor. She ain't gonna have time for any activity like that," Rick answered.

"What about you, Promise? You got a young daughter,

right?"

"Yeah, but hell fucking no, I'll be damn if she gonna be rump shaking in any damn video," Promise said shaking his emphatically.

"I'm feeling you, might as well just start ho'ing and start making some real money," Rick said with a chuckle.

"How you know there's any real money in ho'ing? What you pimpin now?" Laughter erupted throughout the barbershop. "Lemme find out you out all night pimpin'?" Nelson laughed.

"He talking plenty shit, huh Nel?"

"Like Tech would say, that's one hun'red," Nelson laughed.

They walked out of the barbershop so fresh and clean. Squeeze and Promise got in the X5 and jetted out to Long Island to pick up Audrey and her girlfriend. Promise was nervous about Squeeze coming along but he was the only nigga suitable in his mind. Show, that nigga didn't know how to act right when he came around bitches or pussy. Pooh, he was still a young nigga in the mind and heart.

Squeeze wasn't perfect, but the nigga was old enough and Promise thought he'd be the only nigga in the crew acceptable. Squeeze wasn't ugly. He was definitely gentle on the eyes with the ladies and he had some manners - sometimes he got too rowdy. Promise prayed he didn't show his true colors tonight in front of Audrey.

Promise prepared for the night and dressed in purple velour Sean John sweat suit, his wife-beater showing underneath. He was flossing with his chain and white Air Force Ones on his feet. Squeeze was geared up in denim jeans and jacket to match with fresh new beige and white Timberlands on his feet. He was sporting his blue fitted Yankee baseball cap the gangsta hood way, low over his eyes.

They took exit 21 off of Southern State Parkway and drove into Baldwin, Long Island. Promise followed the directions that Audrey gave to him over the phone. Ten minutes later, they pulled up in front of a sprawling Ranch style home with the manicured lawn out front.

"Nice crib," Squeeze uttered.

Promise picked up his cellphone and dialed Audrey's house number from the Jeep.

"Hello?"

"Audrey?"

"Yes."

"It's Promise. We're outside," he informed her.

"Oh. Why don't y'all come in? My homegirl isn't ready yet."

"Ahight," he said clicking off.

"What she say?" Squeeze asked.

"She told us to come in."

Promise was about ready to exit his Jeep when Squeeze said to him, "Hold on."

"What's good, nigga?"

"Why da fuck you bring da gat for?" Promise barked.

"Nigga, I don't know these bitches. You never know," Squeeze said lifting his shirt and revealing his .380.

"It ain't dat kind of party, Squeeze," Promise stated. "Leave dat shit in the car, Squeeze."

Squeeze lifted the gun from out his waistband and hid it under the passenger seat. "You happy, nigga?"

Promise didn't reply. He stepped out and headed toward the front door. Squeeze was just a few steps behind him. They got to the door and before he could ring the bell, Audrey opened the door smiling.

"Hey you," she uttered, cheesing as she peered at Promise. "Who's your friend?"

"Audrey, dis is Squeeze. Squeeze, dis is Audrey," he introduced.

"Hey... Squeeze huh? Where do y'all come up with these names?" She giggled looking at Squeeze. He's cute too, she thought.

"What up, luv," Squeeze said in a deep toned voice.

Promise stared at Audrey and complimented her, "God, you're beautiful. You look nice." He bent down to kiss her on the cheek, inhaling her scent.

"Thank you. You're looking mighty fine yourself too and you smell so good. I like that cologne you have on."

"I can't come to your crib stinking and shit. Gotta smell nice."

Audrey liked that. A nigga thugging like him, looking the way he was and smelling sexy. He was fine.

Audrey had on a denim miniskirt with the shin high boots, a tight white shirt, and her breasts protruded out something lovely. Before they headed out, she threw on her denim jacket. Her sinuous hair fell gracefully down her shoulders. Her beautiful presence lit up the room.

"Where's your friend?" Promise asked.

"Oh, she's in the bathroom. Y'all want something to drink, a snack maybe, while we wait for her?"

"Nah, I'm good," Promise said.

"What about your friend?"

"Nah, I'm good, luv...thanks anyway."

"Well, y'all chill out and give me a minute. Let me go get my friend. She be taking forever sometimes," Audrey said leaving the room.

"Damn, nigga...dats you?" Squeeze asked soon as Audrey was out of their sight.

Promise smiled. "She fine, right?"

"You fucked her yet?"

"Nigga...chill...it ain't even like that."

"Whatever, nigga...you know you want dat. All I know is her friend better be just as fine or I'm gonna embarrass the bitch. I tell you Promise, she better not be coming back out here wit' a fuckin' baboon leaching on her back."

"Nah, she told me her friend is cute. She vouched for her."

"Ahight, nigga...we'll see. I'll be the judge of dat."

They sat and waited for about ten minutes until Audrey stepped back in the room with her friend following right behind her.

"Everyone, this is Camille," Audrey introduced.

Damn! Both men thought at the sight of Camille. Audrey was right she was definitely a cutie. Camille was light-skinned with a slender sexy figure, brown eyes just like her friend, and her breasts a lil' plump, not a handful like Audrey but they were right enough.

She had long braids, freshly done, and they went down her back. She was dressed in a white mock neck and pleated skirt, white stilettos that made the structure of her legs definitely stand out, and her sweet lips were glossed out.

Squeeze was unquestionably impressed by her looks and the way she stared back at him. It was on and poppin'. No regrets here for either of 'em.

They piled into Promise□s X5. Audrey rode shotgun and Camille hopped in the back with Squeeze. Promise drove out to Jimmy's Bronx Café, out in the Bronx. The four of 'em talked, laughed, and cliqued lovely; everyone was feeling everyone.

The ride ended in front of Jimmy's Bronx Cafe around ten thirty. It took Promise ten minutes to find a decent parking spot. Afterwards, the four of 'em strutted into the place looking like two million dollar couples. Audrey walked close to Promise and Camille was next to Squeeze. The host of the restaurant sat the four near the oversized window overlooking the Deegan Expressway. Being the gentlemen that they seemed to be, both men pulled out the chairs for their ladies.

"Thank you," both ladies uttered simultaneously taking a seat.

"This is nice. I never been here before," Camille said glancing around.

Promise and Squeeze sat opposite of each other. Both men looked like true ballers sitting with their attractive dates for the night.

"So, gentlemen, I'm curious. Why do y'all call y'all selves Squeeze and Promise? I know y'all mammas ain't give y'all them names," Camille inquired.

Promise smiled. "Actually, Promise is my middle name. I don't care to disclose my first name at dis time."

"Why, state secret or your mamma gave you a geeky name?"

"Nah, I just don't like a whole lot of folks knowing my government like dat," he explained.

"What about you, Squeeze? I mean, what's that about?"

Squeeze let out a slight chuckle. "I'm wit' my nigga Promise here. Squeeze is what every nigga out there on dem streets know me by and they don't know me by no other name. Dats how I like it and dats how I keep it."

"So, y'all some two gangsta ass niggas, huh?" Audrey joked.

"Nah, we just keep it real," Squeeze said.

The waiter came over and asked if they were ready to order. Promise told him to give 'em a few more minutes. Everyone looked at their menus and tried to decide on what to order. Everything flowed smoothly. Squeeze was behaving and the night looked good.

After everyone gave their orders, the ladies got up to use the restroom. When they were out of sight, Squeeze joked, "Damn, nigga...Audrey gotta pair of balloons stashed under her shirt. You sure you can handle dat by yourself. Her friend Camille is fine though. You know a nigga gotta ease up in dat sometime tonight."

"Behave yourself, Squeeze...don't fuck dis shit up for me," Promise said to him.

"Damn nigga, you really like dat bitch?"

"She's cool people."

"Yeah, whatever. Man, you're just trying to get some pussy. I ain't hating nigga. She a bad ass bitch, though."

Promise smiled. "Chill nigga."

"Nah. I'm cool. I ain't gonna fuck your game up tonight. I'm trying to do me, too." Squeeze glanced back at the restroom to see if the ladies were coming out. When he didn't see 'em; he turned back to Promise and said, "Yo, Promise, let me pull your coat to sump'n."

"What's up, nigga?"

"I'm working on dis deal right now...major money, yo." Squeeze enlightened quietly.

"What you talking about, Squeeze?"

"Look, you my nigga but this stick-up shit we doing, it ain't kicking it anymore. Shit getting too risky for us out there. I've been thinking... I established this connect, right? He got the product but he ain't got the muscle out there to push his shit for him. He needs workers. He need niggas dat know how to handle the streets. He wanna work wit' us, cut us in. Move his weight out there for him and we get dat percentage."

"What you talking about? What kinda weight do he wanna move?"

"Mostly trees and white powder."

"Damn, Squeeze, dats some serious shit."

"Yeah but check dis out. We move in on dem Tompkins Ave niggas and take dey shit over. Dem niggas is weak out there, they can't hold down fort like dat...fuck dat nigga, Nine. We get dat territory poppin' and let niggas know we ain't playin', dat we in charge...and you just watch dat money pour in. I need this long-term money, nigga."

The girls came out the bathroom laughing and headed back to the table.

"What y'all fellas over here talking about?" Audrey asked smiling down at Promise.

"Nuthin', just missing y'all, dats all," Promise said.

"Umm hum, whatever. They probably discussing about our bodies. You know how niggas do, Audrey," Camille said. "You know they been looking."

Squeeze laughed. "Hey, I ain't gonna front. Shit is tight. Is it wrong to notice?"

"As long as the two of you are only noticing me and my girl here for the night we cool," Camille said.

"Luv, we don't even get down like dat," Squeeze mentioned. "Anyway, y'all the two finest ladies in the place. These chickens in here can't fuck wit' y'all."

"I like him," Camille uttered giving him a hug.

"Camille, you're crazy," Audrey chimed in.

The waiter finally arrived with their orders and placed their food gently down in front of them. Everyone started to dine, drink and continue to have a good time. By one in the morning, the girls had enough to eat and the men wanted to move on. Squeeze suggested that they go to the bar located in the back of the restaurant. The night was still young. Everyone got up and started to move to the bar.

"Y'all go on. I gotta make a quick phone call," Promise said.

"Ahight...you know where we at," Squeeze replied heading to where the fun was. Camille was under his arm and Audrey was at his side.

Promise called Ms. Watson's crib to check on his daughter. He waited patiently as the phone rang multiple times before she picked up.

"Hello? Ms. Watson, it's Promise."

"How you doing, sweetie."

"How is she doing? She ain't giving you any trouble?" he asked.

"No, Promise, we had a good time. I put her to bed at 9. Stop worrying yourself and have a good time. I mothered four children and eight grandchildren."

"Thanks Ms. Watson. I appreciate this so much," Promise smiled.

"You're welcome. Now don't be having that girl of yours waitin' too long while you talking to me...enjoy the night."

He hung up and proceeded to the bar where the music was bumping. Squeeze and the girls sat at a small table set up with drinks.

"Sorry about dat. I had to check up on my daughter," he explained.

"Nah, that's cool. We didn't mind," Audrey said smiling at him and definitely feeling his vibe.

They continued drinking. Camille suggested they hit the dance floor because one of her songs was playing. She pulled Squeeze up by his arms gesturing that she wanted to dance. He didn't resist. They began to grind, drawing minor attention to themselves.

Niggas were ogling Camille. She had it going on, hiking up her skirt a bit, her legs gleaming in the dim light, teasing niggas while she gyrated her hips against Squeeze. The both of 'em looked like they were shooting a scene out of Dirty Dancing.

"Your girl's crazy?" Promise stated.

"Hey, that's her...she be bugging sometimes," Audrey explained.

"Well, she got the right nigga to bug out wit'. He crazy too."

"You dance?" Ashley smiled.

"Me? Nah, sometimes I ain't a big dancer."

"That's cool."

"Why? You dance?"

"A little. I don't get down like my girl but I can hold it down," she said.

"Want another drink?" Promise asked.

Audrey nodded and he ordered her a Long Island Iced tea and for himself a Hennessy and Cranberry. The conversation between the two was definitely flowing.

It was almost two in the morning. Promise and Audrey were having a good time until they heard a disturbance near by. He looked over and saw Squeeze getting into an altercation with two males.

Promise rushed up outta his chair and ran over to where they were arguing but before he could get there, Squeeze had smashed a bottle over one guy's head and was cursing and carrying on. A quick fight broke out and Promise had his boy's back. He jumped in and they both got thrown out quickly.

The girls met 'em outside and Audrey, looking shocked but not upset, asked them, "What was that about?"

"Fuck 'em pussy ass niggas. I'll come back to this muthafucka and shoot the shit up...niggas keep fuckin' wit' me!" Squeeze yelled.

"Chill out, nigga," Promise tried to calm his boy down.

"What happened?" Audrey asked again.

Camille spoke up for Squeeze. "They in there just hating on us. That's all."

"Niggas kept bumping into me, yo, while I was dancing wit' shorty then one of dem niggas had the nerve to step up and stare hard at me like it's my fault," Squeeze said.

"Fuck 'em niggas, you be ahight," Promise said.

"So what's next?" Audrey asked.

Promise looked at her surprised that she wasn't telling him to take her ass home. "Oh, y'all still wanna chill."

"Of course," Camille spoke up. "I ain't got a curfew. You got a curfew, Audrey?" she joked.

"No girl. I've been grown for a long time now."

"So, what's up? Where y'all niggas taking us next?" Camille asked sounding eager and up for more fun.

Promise and Squeeze glanced at each other. "Ahight, I know a spot where we can chill."

They jumped back into Promise's X5 and headed out to Brooklyn. They ended up parked by the rest area under the Verrazano Bridge enjoying the picturesque and tranquil view for the night. Squeeze and Camille stayed in the car while Audrey and Promise went out for a walk.

"I'm having such a good time with you tonight," Audrey said.

Promise smiled and returned with, "You cool peoples...I'm having a good time too."

They walked a good ways, staring at the downtown Manhattan skyline and at the Atlantic Ocean, before either spoke again.

"Can I ask you a question?" Audrey asked.

"Go ahead."

"What happened to Ashley's mother if you don't mind me asking?"

"Nah, it's cool. I don't mind." Promise paused then answered her question. "She was killed a few months ago," he somberly explained.

"Oh... I'm so sorry."

"It's cool. I got custody of her now and she's my heart. I can't live a day without her. It was hard at first but I got used to it. We take care of each other."

Audrey smiled as she listened intently.

"What about you? You got any kids?" Promise asked.

"Me... noooo...I'm not ready for children yet."

"Yeah, don't rush it."

"I don't mind taking care of everyone else's children but having a few of my own right now...it's not happening."

"But you want kids sometime in the future, right?"

"Yeah, I want a little boy first because they're easier to raise. Then whatever comes afterwards I'm cool with."

"How many kids do you plan on having?"

"'Bout three. But I don't want three baby daddies...not my style. I plan on getting married first so my husband and I can raise our kids together."

"I like dat. You got standards."

"You got to. Too many fucked up things going on in the world today for females to be going out and getting themselves pregnant twenty-four seven."

"So let me ask you a question," Promise said.

"Go ahead, shoot."

"What kinda men are you attracted to? I mean, not just physically but personality as well?" he asked. "Be honest."

"Um..." Audrey murmured smiling. "I like em tall. I like dark-skinned men. I'm not into light-skinned men. He's gotta be sweet, charming, and chocolate. No, I'm joking, a brother's gotta be responsible."

A smile appeared on Promise's mug while he listened.

"He also gotta be stable and have a sense of humor. I can't stand boring men. I like to have fun."

"I feel you," Promise uttered.

"And his hygiene gotta be on point. I can't stand a nigga

with a stench."

Promise quickly sniffed under his armpits for good measure. Audrey started laughing. "Nah, you're good. You smell fine. Believe me, you wouldn't have made it this far if I wasn't feeling you like that."

"You feeling me, huh?" Promise smiled.

"So far..."

"How far?"

"You got potential. I'll give you that," she stated.

"Ahight, ahight...that's cool. I'm feelin' you too, girl."

"I know," she replied.

"Look at you, all confident."

"A woman's gotta be confident in today's society."

"I like," Promise said quietly.

"You like what?" she said.

"Your assertiveness."

"Lemme find out you using all them big words," Audrey joked.

"I'm not that stupid, I can see when you're playin' round with me," Promise joked.

"Yeah. I see that..."

They continued kicking it as the walked. Suddenly they stopped after realizing that they'd walked some distance because of how involved they'd been in their conversation. They decided to turn back.

After a moment's silence, Promise unexpectedly blurted out, "Jayson!"

"Excuse me?"

"My first name is Jayson. I thought you should know."

"Jayson, huh, not a bad name. Cute, I like Promise better.

It's endearing and unique."

"Thanks."

"So, Promise, you don't mind if I ask you something else?"

"Nah, go ahead...shoot away."

"What do you do for a living?"

Now that question caught Promise off guard. He wasn't expecting her to ask about his personal income so soon. He was scared to be honest, fearing the worst; if he said he was a stick-up kid in Brooklyn plus a drug-dealer, it would drive her off.

They stopped walking. "Be honest with me, Promise," Audrey insisted.

Promise stared into her warm brown eyes and couldn't look away. At this point, it would be hard to lie.

"Audrey, on the real," he began to speak, "I do me and doing me is sump'n I ain't too thrilled about right now," he deadpanned.

"Oh, really?"

"I do what I gotta do to maintain. I'm taking care of my daughter and myself at the same time."

"You're honest at least. I like that."

"I'm sorry."

"For what?"

"For not being truly real wit' you. I'm scared if I told you everything about me, you wouldn't wanna deal wit' me no more," he explained.

"Listen...I like you and I wanna continue to see you. You're cool," she smiled. "But I'm not about to be all up in your business, at least not right away. You got your daughter to take care of and maintain and what you do with' your boy Squeeze...I know it's hard out there for a bro but think about that little girl in your life."

"Always, Ashley comes first. I thought about getting a job but I ain't got the sweetest background. I got priors on my record."

"Damn, baby," Audrey softly sighed.

Hearing Audrey call him baby perked his ears up a little.

"You know what? I refuse to see another black man destroy himself out there. Especially when he got a beautiful baby girl to take care of. I got family that may be willing to help you out with a gig."

"Gig?"

"A job."

"But you don't know me like that," Promise protested.

"I feel you're a respectful, charming and wonderful man who got caught up with the wrong people doing the wrong things," she said pulling him gently closer to her by his shirt as she backed against the metal railing that separated them from the sea. Promise didn't resist.

"Why you looking out for me?" he asked quietly.

"Because I know a good man when I see one and I can't let you fall, especially after meeting Ashley. You need to stand strong." She moved towards him until their bodies became intertwined and their lips locked against each other. They stood, kissing passionately beneath the stars and the near-by bridge. Promise clutched Audrey tightly and didn't want to let her go. He felt that he could hold onto her forever. She was a blessing!

Promise had a hunch that things were going to be different for him now that he met Audrey. He thanked God for bringing this angel into his life. He needed her and his daughter needed her too.

He drove Audrey and Camille back to Long Island around four that morning. Promise kissed Audrey passionately once more and then drove Squeeze back to Brooklyn.

Over the next few weeks Promise and Audrey became closer spending so much quality-time with each other and Ashley that they felt like family. For once, Audrey made Promise forget about his peoples and troubles in Brooklyn. He was having fun and he didn't want it to ever end. Summertime was around the corner and they had so much planned.

Audrey persuaded her uncle out in Long Island to set Promise up with a summer gig selling cars at a used BMW lot. If her uncle liked the way he performed and if he did a good job then he might put Promise on fulltime. Promise was down for it since he pushed an X5 and BMW's were one of his favorite types of cars.

The chemistry was explosive and popping. Promise had never met a woman like Audrey who looked out for him the way she did. He was in love with her. The most important thing was that Ashley loved Audrey too. It got to the point where he began considering marriage, and this was after knowing her for only two short months.

Promise knew that he had to choose between two families, his street-life and girlfriend. He had practically grown up with Squeeze. They'd been like brothers since they were young along with Pooh and Show. Squeeze had always looked out for Promise when Promise needed money.

When he had beef, Squeeze was there. Anything Promise needed or any problems he had, Squeeze, Pooh and Show had always been there. His niggas from Brooklyn had become like a surrogate family to him over the years.

Now Promise felt that he had a new family in his life. Audrey and her peeps looked out for him in a way that was safer and socially acceptable. He got a job for the summer, so that kept his ass out of Brooklyn and out of trouble. Audrey was always around. When Promise needed someone to talk to, Audrey was there to listen. When he had a problem, she was there especially when it came to his daughter. Audrey became a surrogate mother for Ashley.

Who was he more devoted to? Was it his niggas that he had known for life, or Audrey, the angel who had come into his life and had became a major driving force in his existence? It was either the streets or his *sweet.*

It was late June and Promise was laid up in between Audrey's thick brown skinned thighs, enjoying her womanly bliss. He was stroking his manhood submissively inside her as he grunted and clutched her sheets. He'd been at her place for the entire weekend while Ashley stayed with Ms. Watson. They needed some alone time.

Audrey lived with her mother but her mom was never home and the mom had also taken a liking to Promise and Ashley. It was always a pleasure for her to have them both come over.

It had been almost two-weeks since Promise had hung with Squeeze and the others. His time was caught up with Audrey. It felt good to get away from the streets, the drama, the problems and headaches of Brooklyn, New York. Long Island was tranquil and passive. It provided an escape from Brooklyn where there was constant traffic and it was so congested with people and problems.

Each time he visited Brooklyn, he noticed the constant gunshots echoing even more. Although he used to have an apartment out here, now for the first time, he felt removed. When he looked around in L.I., this was a place where he'd love to raise his daughter. Far Rockaway, Queens wasn't that much of a better place for Ashley to live. It wasn't Brooklyn but it was still the ghetto and they had their ways too.

It was eleven on a Sunday night when Promise's cellphone began ringing off the hook. He tried to ignore it but something told him to answer it. Audrey asked him to put it on vibrate or to turn it completely off but he disregarded her suggestion. He finally answered after the umpteenth ring.

"Nigga, where da fuck you at?" Squeeze shouted, his voice guttural. "I've been trying to reach you all night."

"I'm busy," Promise explained. "Why.... what's going on?"

"Pooh got shot!" Squeeze bluntly said.

"What?" Promise uttered as he rose out of bed and released himself from Audrey's precious grip. He rested his back against the headboard. Hearing that Pooh got shot suddenly bought him out of the paradise he'd escaped to for the past two-weeks. "When?"

"We need you out here, Promise."

"Okay, I'm on my way… where y'all niggas at?"

"We at Kings County hospital," Squeeze informed him.

"Ahight, I'll be there soon." Promise hung up and rushed outta bed. He began searching for his clothes.

"Promise…who was that? What happened?" Audrey asked looking worried.

"I gotta go, Audrey. Sump'n came up."

"I'm coming too."

"Nah, you need to stay here."

"I know you're going out to Brooklyn. Promise, what happened?" she asked jumping out of bed naked. She began searching for her clothing.

"You can't come wit' me, Audrey…it's too dangerous out there for you."

"Promise, tell me what happened!"

"A friend of mine was shot tonight," he dryly explained as he threw on his Timberlands.

"Omigod! Is he all right?"

"I don't know."

Promise was fully dressed and 'bout ready to head out when Audrey grabbed his arm. She looked gravely worried. "Don't go, please."

"Audrey, I gotta go. I gotta see what went down."

"There's nothing out there for you anymore, Promise. You need to stop thinking about those friends of yours who are gonna get you killed one day and start thinking about us and your daughter. You start your new job next week."

"These are my niggas, Audrey. They've been looking out for me forever and I gotta see what happened."

"Promise, if you go out there… they gonna get you in some shit."

"Audrey, I can take care of myself. I gotta go see my nigga Pooh and find out what went down," Promise said.

"I'm coming."

"No!" Promise shouted. "I don't want you out there. It's not your world. I gotta go on my own. I promise you, Audrey, dat I ain't gonna get into no shit," he assured her staring into her eyes.

Audrey's eyes began welling up with tears. Her woman's intuition told her that if Promise left her side and went out to Brooklyn, something terrible was about to happen. Audrey had never felt so strongly for a man before and she didn't want to lose Promise so soon.

Promise pulled himself away and walked briskly to the front door. Audrey followed behind staring helplessly out her living room window, watching him as he got into his Jeep and drove off hastily. She collapsed on the couch, tears trickling down. She worried for his safety as he made his way to Brooklyn to meet up with friends that he had just said were too dangerous to be around.

She whispered a silent prayer and begged God for her man's safe return.

Promise arrived at Kings County Hospital a little after midnight. He didn't care where he parked. He just jumped outta his X5 and dashed into the emergency room where he was greeted by Squeeze and Show.

"Where he at?" Promise asked.

Show, a somber expression on his face, bowed and shook his head. From that, Promise knew the deal.

"Da nigga's dead!" Squeeze straightforwardly told him.

Promise shook his head. "Stop playin'…what da fuck happened?" he asked staring directly at Squeeze. He knew Squeeze had the answer to Pooh's death.

"Da nigga, Nine, yo…he gotta go," Squeeze yelled.

"What…Nine shot Pooh?"

"Da nigga gotta go, Promise…he disrespected us, yo…dem niggas from Tompkins Ave killed Pooh. They gotta get got, yo."

"Squeeze, I'm down," Show chimed in.

"What happened?" Promise asked again.

"Fuck you mean, what happened? Pooh's lying dead and you standing here all nonchalant like Pooh's death don't mean shit," Squeeze shouted. "Da bitch from L.I. got you soft, huh? You suppose to fuck dat bitch and let her be - like I did her friend. We suppose to be family; niggas know each other since we knee high. Don't put a bitch before your niggas. You should be ready to murder right now! Ask what da fuck happened later, nigga. You gonna be down wit' your niggas who had your back for life or you gonna diss us for some bitch you don't even know like that?"

The intensity in Squeeze's eyes let Promise know that if he wasn't down tonight, there was going to be beef between him and Squeeze later. Show and Squeeze glared at him waiting for his reply. Promise knew that Squeeze was upset because of Pooh's death and that was why he was trippin' like that.

Promise's conscience ran wild while he rode in the back of Squeeze's truck on the way to Tompkins Ave to get retaliation for their man. Promise had known this day was inevitable; today he had to prove himself to the crew and take a life for a life for their fallen brother, Pooh.

It had come down to a choice between his loyalty to the streets and his niggas or becoming a family with the girl he loved. Promise thought on this as he gripped the black nine-millimeter in his hand, his heart beating rapidly, palms sweating, mind racing as he peered out the passenger window.

Ashley and Audrey had become the two most important people in his life right now. So, why was he in this truck on his way to commit murder? He had a future, yet here he was traveling down a Brooklyn street with Brooklyn niggas ready to commit a few 187's on this hot June summer night.

The truck was quiet, everyone deep in thought. Show drove while Squeeze rode shotgun. Promise's cellphone rang insistently with Audrey's special ring. The calls went straight to voicemail.

It was 1a.m. and hot outside. July 4th was right around the corner. Everyone was still outside their apartments, drinking, socializing, smoking and a few hustlers out still operating business— business as in the drug dealers were still out in the court yards and lobbies treating and feeding their coke and dope addicted fiends through the morning hours. It was 95 degrees and the unfortunate residents in the building without air-conditioning had decided to keep cool by staying out of their sweltering apartments trying to catch a night breeze.

Nine and his cronies were also out, chilling and mingling in front of their place of business on Tompkins and Myrtle in front of the building where their customers could find them easy.

Squeeze's truck slowly turned the corner with its headlights off. They quickly spotted Nine and his peeps. Show put the truck in park and shut off the ignition.

"Fuck dat, we just gonna run up on these niggas," Squeeze said cocking back his weapon and stepping outta the truck. Show followed and Promise was the last to exit.

Squeeze wanted to run up on these niggas and murder them all. He didn't give a fuck how many heads were out at one in the morning. As far as he was concerned, he was taking and making it his business. The beef between Nine and Squeeze became personal when they killed Pooh.

They slowly crept up to Nine and his peeps with their guns out and held down to their side advancing quickly and quietly toward their targets. Before they could get up on them, the element of surprise was lost when one of Nine's men spotted the attack coming and shouted out, "Nine, look-out," while drawing his .45 and firing into the night.

Squeeze and Show quickly returned fire. Promise became startled, ducked and then he returned fire. His life was in danger. Rapid gunfire echoed out into the night and folks and residents who were out just trying to enjoy the summer night quickly dashed to take cover from the gunshots riddling the projects.

Promise let off multiple rounds at six men firing at him. He didn't see Squeeze or Show as he darted into the street, bullets whizzing by his ears. He felt alone; he knew he was on his own. It wasn't about revenge now; it was about survival. They were outgunned and outnumbered. Police sirens pierced the air.

When Promise saw the blue and white cop cars rushing in with the overhead blue and red lights blaring repetitively, he panicked and fired at the first oncoming squad car striking the cop in the passenger seat in his chest. The driver got out when his partner was hit by a bullet he returned fire. But Promise had already taken off running.

He sprinted through the projects with his gun still in hand, scared to drop his weapon, fearing the cops would find it and trace his fingerprints back to him. Having his gun on him was too risky so when Promise came to a nearby corner, he dropped his gun down a sewer drain and continued running.

Promise heard the wailing police sirens. He tried not to panic and look suspicious and to stay out of the cops' sight knowing that if they saw him sweating, exhausted, and not too far from the crime scene, it was his ass. Promise would see Central Booking tonight and probably jail for a long, long time if he got caught.

He crept his way through the night, trying to be as inconspicuous as possible. Beads of sweat trickled down his face. Promise couldn't stop shaking. He thought about his daughter and Audrey. He needed to get out of Brooklyn fast. He had shot a cop and the police would be harassing every young black male in the vicinity.

Promise stumbled upon a cabstand and ducked behind a parked car when police cars suddenly raced by. After the area cleared, he darted into the cabstand and told the dispatcher that he needed a cab fast. There was a cab on hand in five minutes.

Promise jumped in and told the driver his location. He needed to get back to King's County to get his ride where he'd left it parked and bounce outta Brooklyn and back to Queens or L.I.

It was three in the morning when Audrey heard a loud knock and the constant ringing of the bell at her front door. Luckily she was home alone or her moms would've been very upset at the sudden disturbance at the front door so early in the morning. She wasn't asleep. She had been up since Promise left. He'd been gone for four hours so when she heard the loud knocks, Audrey silently prayed. Deep inside she felt something was wrong.

She scurried to the door in her house robe and slippers and relief surged through her when she peeped outside. Promise came flying in, sweaty and bleeding.

"Ohmigod! Baby, what happened?" Audrey cried panic-stricken.

go-getter girl

MARK ANTHONY

I had never walked a day in his shoes so I couldn't start judging the man. Yeah, I was pissed that he hadn't listened to me and stayed his ass home for the night but this definitely wasn't the time for me to start throwing it up in his face. Promise was scared and I needed to let him know that I was there for him no matter what!

"Promise, calm down and tell me exactly what happened," I stated coming across like a concerned mother. Promise was breathing heavy as he picked himself up from off of my living room floor.

"Baby, I can't really tell you more than I already told you... I shot a cop! It was crazy! Shit just happened," Promise shook his head.

"Promise, I can help you but if you don't tell me everything then I won't know how to help you!"

"Audrey, listen. You already know too much. My world and your world are two completely different worlds. If the cops catch wind that I did this and they come questioning people... I don't wanna put you in a position where you would have to lie for me. You kna'I'mean? You can't tell nobody more than what you know. So, if I don't tell you everything...You get the picture?"

I understood where Promise was coming from but he had me all wrong. He was right that we came from two different worlds but he was wrong if he thought that I would just sell him out because he'd made a mistake.

"Promise, look at me! Look at me in my eyes," I instructed as I stood there in my silk robe and slippers trying to persuade him to trust me.

He tilted his head slightly to the right. He bit his bottom lip and I could see the tension in his face as he listened. His eyes were fixated on mine.

"Obviously I don't know what it feels like to shoot a cop. But I can tell you this; my head is a whole lot clearer than yours so I'm in a position to think more logically than you. Trust me, baby! Tell me exactly what happened and let me try help you figure this thing out."

I must have broken through the wall that Promise had erected because he sighed real heavy and looked as though he were prepared to say something but the words just wouldn't come out.

"Promise, trust me. It's not about you and me. I know how much you love your daughter and how real she is to you. I'm not gonna steer you wrong for her sake."

He gripped the top of his head with the palms of both hands and slowly slid his palms down his face stopping at his chin as though he were trying to wipe away the anguish he was experiencing.

"Ahight, see this is what happened. My man Pooh was the one that got shot."

"Oh God!" I responded in shock simply because I knew how close Promise was to Pooh, "Is he ok?"

"Nah, the nigga died on the operating table in the Trauma unit!" Promise stated with tears welling up in his eyes although as he proceeded to explain the chain of events he didn't shed one tear.

"We knew the cats that shot him were them punk ass niggas from Bed-Stuy! That was our man and all! So we brought it to them. We drove to their spot and ran up on them niggas and starting firing! It was crazy 'cause them niggas didn't see us coming until the last minute but when they saw us, their whole crew pulled out burners and started bustin' back at us. Next thing

I knew I got separated from Squeeze and Show. I was dodging bullets left and right. I was buggin' 'cause I thought I was gonna get hit but I just kept firing at anybody and everybody. At that point I was just trying to stay alive."

I didn't want to interrupt Promise but I had to butt in and ask a question, "So Promise, please tell me that Squeeze and Show are ok...Are they?"

"I don't know! Word is bond! Like I said, things jumped off so quick and then we got separated. There was shots ringing out every which way so I really don't know if them niggas is dead or alive...I was gonna call them on their cells but didn't 'cause if them niggas was hiding out from the cops or whatever I didn't wanna get them busted by having their cellphones ringing and giving them away. So while I was running through the projects trying to stay alive, I started hearing sirens. Five-O was coming up every block. There were marked units and unmarked units driving the wrong way up one-way streets and all of that. I saw a marked unit and it looked like they were coming right for me 'cause dude driving the car was doing like 80 miles an hour up on the sidewalk! So when I saw that, I panicked. I had the toast in my hand and just fired!"

"At the cops?" I asked in disbelief.

"Yeah, it was more of a automatic reflex. I didn't wanna get caught with the gun but at the same time I didn't wanna toss it just in case I had to buss back at them niggas that was bustin' at me, and especially since I lost my peoples. I was going for dolo. I definitely couldn't just toss the gun."

Promise stopped and I urged him on, "Keep on. So you fired at the cops and then what?"

"I'm almost sure that it was the first shot that hit one of

the cops in the chest. It went right through the passenger side windshield and caught the cop on the passenger side like pow! So the cop that was driving, he slams on the brakes and gets out, kneels in position and starts firing at me but I stayed low and just hauled my ass deeper into the projects until I found a spot where I could just dip out and walk out on one of the side streets like everything was everything. At that point, the cops were more worried about the cop that got hit than they were about catching me so that gave me like a minute or two to slip them."

"So did you leave in your car or what? I mean you still were all alone right?"

"Yeah, I was still alone...What I did was I tossed the gun in this sewer and made it to a cab stand then hopped into a cab and took the cab back to my car which wasn't even in Bed-Stuy. It was still parked at the hospital, Kings County hospital...So after I got in my whip, I headed straight back here to your crib... Audrey it was crazy! Word! On the real, I don't know how I'm not dead! But thank God I made it outta there alive."

I took in all that he had told me. I had to pinch myself to see if this was real or not because what he had described sounded like something I read about in the newspaper. At the same time, I had to admit that a part of me was attracted to that whole gangsta lifestyle and the story that he had told me was actually turning me on in a *sick* kind of way. I guess it's because that whole gangsta world is so taboo since I had never ran with a real thug before. Maybe it's human nature to be attracted to the unfamiliar, I don't know.

What I do know is that Promise had just survived a wild shoot out and he had the balls enough to shoot a cop. So if he could live through that and survive, then it would be nothing for me to stick by him and help him navigate through these streets as a wanted fugitive on the run. He was street and there was no sense in me trying to make him into something that he was not.

By this time, Promise and I were both sitting on my living room couch. I leaned close to him and I gave him a reassuring hug. Promise held on to me for dear life. His body felt so good and tight I began to get aroused. I kept telling him everything was gonna be alright. Promise looked at me and then I made the move to kiss him. I wanted the kiss to last longer than it did but I knew that even though I was getting hornier by the minute, this wasn't the time to stick my tongue down his throat.

My practical side took over. "Promise, call Ms. Watts and let her know that I'm coming by to pick up Ashley," I instructed as I took off my robe in preparation to get dressed.

"Now?" Promise questioned.

"Yeah, right now!" I demanded as I searched for some shoes.

"Audrey, it's four in the morning! I'll get her at like 12 noon. And if you don't mind, after I pick her up, can Ashley and me just chill with you for one night? I just need one night to figure out what to do."

"Promise, you're not listening to me. I need to go get your daughter right now! You sitting there talking about getting her this afternoon. Are you buggin?"

See, this is exactly what I had been trying to tell Promise. He had just shot a cop and he wasn't in a position to think straight. His nerves and adrenaline were thinking for him. I, on the other hand, was his voice of reason so I had to assert myself and let him know exactly what it was that needed to be done and why.

"Okay Promise, tell me this. The sewer that you tossed

the gun in, was it one of those sewers that is packed to the brim with garbage or was it filled with water?"

"Baby, I don't even know. I just tossed it and kept it moving."

"Promise, listen. We gotta assume that the sewer, if it's like most New York City sewers, then it was packed with garbage. That means that the cops probably have that gun as we speak! They're probably lifting the prints off of the gun and with your priors...Come on, Promise, put it together!"

Promise looked at me and knew that I was dead on point with what I was saying. I continued, "For all you know, Squeeze and Show could be in the precinct right now ratting you out! I'm not saying that they're rats, I'm just trying to get you to see the big picture. And baby, the big picture is this; if we turn on the TV news right now and find out that that cop is dead, you best believe that every cop in the city is hunting you down right now. I can guarantee you that they are looking for every possible clue to try and figure out who in the hell shot one of their boys!"

I didn't want Promise to panic but he was beginning to do just that so I had to quickly calm him down.

"Promise, just relax and listen to me! The reason I have to go get Ashley now is because the cops are probably on their way to your building as we speak. And if they aren't there now, you better believe that a whole sea of them will be by the time day breaks."

"You're exactly right!" Promise stated as he began pacing back and forth in Tims that were scuffed and filthy during the shootout.

I handed Promise the cordless telephone and demanded he call Ms. Watts. While upstairs in my room and dressing, I could hear him explaining to Ms. Watts that "a woman by the name of Audrey" would be coming by to get Ashley in fifteen or twenty minutes. From the way Promise was speaking, I could tell that Ms. Watts must've been alarmed but thank God, Promise pressed the issue and insisted that she prepare Ashley to get picked up right away.

Promise was off the phone by the time I made it back to the living room. I had thrown on a Sean John sweat suit with sneakers and no socks.

"I'm gonna take my mother's car. What building is Ms. Watts in and what's her apartment number?" I asked.

"Nah, I'm a roll with you," Promise stated.

"Promise, I'm going alone! No one is here at my crib so just chill and relax until I get back. It's gonna be ahight…"

Promise didn't put up a fight. He nodded and said, "Ahight, she lives in the building directly across from mine in apartment 2J."

I grabbed the car keys from off the kitchen table, giving Promise a kiss on the cheek, "When I get in the car I'll call you on my cellphone. When you hear the house phone ring, just pick it up 'cause it'll be me, ok."

Promise nodded his head and I left. As I started up my mother's Jeep Cherokee and pulled off, I remember asking myself what in the world I was doing? But what I reasoned and told myself is that I was simply helping out a friend. Yeah, he was a friend with benefits. I would always look out for anyone I'm true-friends with. That's the kind of person I am. I reached forward and adjusted the car radio so that I could tune into AM radio - 1010 WINS, 24-7 news radio.

As I turned up the volume on the radio, the breaking news

was about the cop that had been shot in Brooklyn, the same cop Promise had shot. My heart rate increased as I listened and heard the reporter tell how the rookie police officer had died while being rushed to Brookdale Hospital.

The reporter explained that they had one suspect in custody and that the Police department had virtually "locked down" that entire area in Brooklyn in order to comb the area and search for the murder weapon as well as other suspects. Police officers from across the city were doing an apartment by apartment and a floor-by-floor search of the entire housing project complex in which the officer had been shot.

I immediately drove a little faster in order to get my ass to Far Rockaway to pick up Ashley. As I pressed down harder on the accelerator and quickly navigated through the dark and barren early morning New York streets, I dialed my house so that I could speak to Promise. Promise picked up on the first ring.

"Hello."

"Promise, it's me. You okay?"

"Yeah, I'm good. I'm just sitting here wondering how the hell did I get mixed up in all this."

"Baby, listen. Things just got a helluva lot thicker!"

"Why, what's up? Is something wrong with Ashley?" Promise nervously questioned. "No baby, nothing like that. I just turned on the radio and I found out that the cop that got shot, he died on the way to the hospital."

"Say word!"

"Yeah, they said he got shot in the collar bone just above his bullet proof vest but the bullet traveled inside his body and hit a major artery."

After those words left my mouth, there was dead silence

on the other end of the phone.

"Promise? Promise are you there?"

"Yeah, yeah, I'm here. I'm thinking. Yo, baby, I gotta get up outta New York for a minute. These streets of New York is gonna be too hot and I ain't trying to get bagged in my own backyard!"

"Baby, listen, first of all, you ain't getting bagged so stop talking that foolishness. Just relax and I'll be back with Ashley in like a half hour. When I get back, we'll talk. I'll figure this thing out."

"Okay," Promise said, finally sounding as if he trusted me.

"Oh, by the way, have you heard from Squeeze or Show?"

"No, not yet. Why? What do you think?"

"Well, the news did say that one suspect got arrested and that they were searching that entire area looking for other suspects and looking for the murder weapon."

"God damn! There's probably police dogs, helicopters, and the whole nine yards! I know they're gonna find that burner. I should've never tossed it!"

"But Promise, nobody can connect you to me so you're good for now. They won't be able to find you. Just don't call Squeeze or Show. If your cell rings, don't pick it up just let it go to voice mail. Okay?"

"Yeah, yeah, no doubt, baby."

"I'm down with you and we're gonna be okay."

"Audrey, on the real, I love you. Thank you. You looking out for me better than a damn lawyer. And that's peace right there!"

I made it over to Ms. Watts and picked up Ashley. Ashley

looked so cute and innocent as she slept. From the time I took her from Ms. Watts and put her in the car, she never awoke. She stayed asleep the entire ride back to Long Island. Ashley was like most kids that could sleep through a plane crash. As peaceful as she looked, I couldn't help but think how she was so clueless as to the chaos that was surrounding her.

I knew that by helping Promise, I was an accessory to murder and when I thought about Ashley, my heart melted and went out to her. She had no control over her mother getting killed nor over who her daddy was, regardless if he was guilty of murdering a cop. I felt this "motherly" need to protect Ashley and convinced myself that I would literally ride or die with Promise for Ashley's sake.

I made it back to my crib and as I pulled into the driveway, the sun was just about coming up. Promise met me at the front door and took his sleeping daughter from my arms.

"Take her into my room. She can sleep on my bed. The sun is up and I don't think I'm going back to sleep anytime soon."

Promise did as I instructed and when he returned, we made our way into my kitchen.

"Audrey, why are you looking out for me like this? Be real."

As I prepared to cook something for us, I glanced at the man I love then spoke, "Promise, two months ago, on that first night that we went out, remember when we were walking near the Verrazano Bridge?"

"Of course I remember that."

"But do you remember what I said to you?"

"Well, we spoke about a few different things that night."

"What I'm getting at is this: That night, I saw your potential.

When you told me the truth I promise you I'd – I'd help you stand strong... When I said all that I really meant it! I can't explain this heavy connection I feel to you and how real it is! Aside from my mother, this connection feels realer than any emotional connection I've ever had before with anyone."

Promise smiled uncomfortably, his head at a slight angle staring into my eyes making my heartbeat faster. He slowly shook his head.

"What?" I asked smiling and cracking open another egg. "Let me guess. You think that I'm just running game on you or something?"

"Nah, you wanna know what I was really smiling about?"

"Yeah, fill me in," I said as I began to scramble the eggs I had just beaten, with some salt and pepper, while browning the onions.

"It's just jokes so don't beat me up for saying this but, damn! I must really have a magic-stick!'" Promise began laughing.

I stopped beating the egg and smiled widely, "No you didn't just say that! Oh so in spite of all, you still got jokes!"

I was glad that he had chosen to interject some humor into our serious issues.

"I'll give you a pass on that comment," I said then added, "But actually you do have that magic-stick." I began laughing along with him.

When I was done amusing myself, I stated, "Seriously though, it's more than just good sex...Promise, it's something much deeper than that."

Later that day, Promise and I went to visit my uncle who owns the used BMW car lot. We didn't go to talk about the job but we did go to talk business.

See, I knew that my uncle had a past filled with criminal activity. He had been on the straight and narrow for the past ten years but I knew that based on his personal history with gangster life he would be able to relate to Promise.

When we arrived, I introduced Promise to my uncle Brandon and I told him that Promise would no longer need the job but that he did need a big favor. I decided to just let Promise do the talking and ask for the favor himself so that I didn't screw things up.

"So, what's on your mind young blood?" My uncle asked Promise.

"Well, Brandon, I'm a be straight up with you. I got myself into some big trouble with the law and I gotta skip town for a minute. There's probably a warrant out for my arrest and it's like this; I drive a flashy X5 that's registered in my name and I'm not trying to get pulled over by the police and in the process get bagged for an outstanding warrant."

"Okay, I follow you son but how can I help you?"

"I wanna give you the X5 and in return I want you to give Audrey one of your best 325 BMW's. Register it in her name and all that. But I don't want you to resell the X5. I want you to chop it and sell the parts. I know that'll be a lot of work for you but in the end, you'll get more money from chopping the X5 than any of the

325's on this lot are worth!"

My uncle Brandon placed a toothpick in the corner of his mouth and twirled while deep in thought. He scoped Promise up and down trying to look right into his soul. My uncle then turned to me before finally speaking up.

"No dice. Look young blood, you see this young lady right here? She's like a daughter to me. She ain't never been in no trouble before and I'm not trying to see anything happen to her. I definitely ain't trying to see her catch a charge on the count of you. I understand your situation but I'm not co-signing on that. Like I said, no dice."

I wanted to jump in and speak up but Promise spoke before I could form my words.

"Okay, no problem. I respect that and I understand where you're coming from," Promise said as he reached out and gave my uncle a pound.

"Wait a minute."

I jumped in, suddenly very aware that Uncle Brandon was staring at me. As workers and customers milled around the lot, I spoke on my man's behalf.

"Uncle Brandon, for as long as you've known me I never once asked for anything. Then when my mom died you told me if I ever needed anything not to hesitate to ask for it. You told me that when I was thirteen years old and now that I'm twenty-two, I wanna believe that your offer is still on the table. I know you don't know Promise and because you know me, I want you to please, just trust me on this! If somebody were forcing my hand on this I would reach out to you and have you handle it for me. I'm telling you this idea to chop the X5, is our idea. I'm co-signing on it and I'm asking you to co-sign on it for us."

My uncle took two steps away from us and he glanced over to look at something that was happening on the lot. He then turned back to us and paused before he spoke.

"Young blood, leave the car here with me. I'm a take care of it. But let me explain something to you and trust these words 'cause I say what I mean and I mean what I say! I've done more years in the joint than you've been alive. So it's nothing for me to go back. My record show it don't mean nothing to me to kill niggas with these two hands for showing me the smallest bit of disrespect. If you slip up and get my niece caught in some bullshit rap or if you disrespect her in the slightest way, God help yo ass. I don't know what you got going down and I don't wanna know but I do know that if I see any police coming around here sniffing and checking around then that also will be yo ass. You see how calm I'm talking? That's because what I'm saying is not a threat, it's straight up the truth. Ain't nobody more OG than me and I won't hesitate to bring it to your young ass so you better know what the hell you doing, young blood."

The whole deal went smooth with my uncle. He took the X5 and he gave me a late model black 325. He took care of the registration, the plates, and inspection. With his connections at the DMV and with insurance agents, he was able to get it done within a matter of hours so that helped out a whole lot 'cause things had begin to heat up something crazy!

Promise's cellphone had been ringing off the easy. The

majority of the calls Promise recognized as being from either Squeeze or Show. Promise put his phone on speaker mode and played one of the messages that Squeeze had left while I listened in.

"Yo, where you at, nigga? I'm making sure that you good. I hope you ain't get bagged. Call me back nigga! It's Squeeze. Hey, yo, Nine and them stupid niggas shot a cop when we ran up on them. Them niggas is so fuckin' stupid! One!"

After Promise finished, I immediately told him to not even think about calling back Squeeze or Show. How would Squeeze know that Nine and his crew were responsible for shooting the cop? That was probably game. The cops could be making him leave a message like that. I didn't trust anyone. In fact, I had Promise call Nextel's customer service and totally disconnect the service. For the time being that he needed to totally distance himself from anything that could help the cops catch him. The last thing that he needed was a damn cellphone tripping him up.

Things began to heat up something crazy. The cops had found the murder weapon and it was all over the news that the police were running ballistics tests on the gun they had found to determine if it was the murder weapon used to kill the officer. The police also reported how close they were to releasing a photo of the lead suspect believed to be the shooter in the murder of the cop.

We really felt the heat when Ms. Watts had called Promise just prior to him disconnecting his cellphone with Nextel. As he spoke to Ms. Watts, I stood nearby and from the gist of the conversation I could tell what was going on. I became so pissed off with myself I wanted to kick myself for being so stupid! I couldn't believe I had slipped up that way.

When Promise got off the phone, he immediately began telling me what Ms. Watts had said, "Yo, the cops were just at Ms. Watts' crib asking if she'd seen me!"

"I could tell that from the flow of the conversation. What did she say?"

"Well, she was all freaked out. She said that they had a search warrant and that they came in like gangbusters tearing the place apart looking for my ass. She said they told her that I had killed a cop and that if she knew anything about where I was she had better tell them or she could risk getting locked up as an accessory!"

I shook my head thinking about what to do next. Promise was nervous as hell. I had slipped up by having Promise tell Ms. Watts my real name and exactly who I was. How stupid! I should've told him to tell Ms. Watts some fake name and we would've been ahight. Then the cops would have no way of connecting me to Promise. But now...!

"Did she say tell them anything?"

"Nah, she don't know where I'm at but..."

I interrupted him and finished for him, "But she told them that a woman named Audrey came by in the wee hours of the morning and picked up his daughter."

Promise paced the floor and I could see the anguish on his face. "Promise, I'm sorry. I should have told you to give Ms. Watts a fake name for me when I went to pick up Ashley."

"Audrey, what the hell are you apologizing for?" Promise shouted, "If it wasn't for you insisting that Ashley get picked up right away then who knows what would have happened. I mean I would've got knocked going to pick her up."

Promise began to take charge and assert himself. "Yo, we

were one step ahead of the cops by picking up Ashley when we did and now we just gotta stay one step ahead of them now. After they left Ms. Watts they probably headed straight to the daycare center. How is it gonna look when they get to the daycare center and find out that Ashley is absent on the same day that her teacher named *Audrey* called in sick?"

"But, Promise, that ain't nothing 'cause I was only a temporary worker there. If I never go back to that job, it won't mean nothing."

"Yeah, but that's neither here nor there. What I am getting at is that the cops are gonna follow every lead. They could be on their way to your crib right now! Baby, we gotta bounce! Go upstairs and get Ashley. I know what we gonna do but I need you to ride with me."

"Promise, you know I'm riding with you!"

Without hesitation, I grabbed Ashley and the three of us quickly jumped in the 325 and made our way onto the Southern State Parkway. As we drove, I was thinking that we might be heading to a hotel or something. I didn't know if Promise had any money on him but it was ok because I had my credit card and about $300 in my bag so I figured my cash alone would be enough to cover the hotel expenses for a day or two. If we needed more then I'd just use my plastic.

"Audrey, get off at the Linden Blvd exit in Elmont," Promise instructed.

"Exit 13?" I curiously asked while thinking to myself that there weren't any hotels or motels in that area.

"Yeah, I gotta make a quick stop at the bank," Promise nonchalantly replied.

"Nah, I got money. I got $300 on me. You don't need

no ATM machines. With the cameras the cops could trace the transactions."

"I'm good. Don't worry about it. Just get off at Linden Blvd and go to ECSB."

I didn't like Promise's idea of stopping at a bank but did as I was instructed. I exited off the parkway and pulled into the first parking space I saw which was half block away from the East Coast Savings Bank. Promise got out and he told me that he'd be right back.

As I watched him walk his sexy ass into the bank, I couldn't help notice how nice the weather was. Unfortunately, when you're on the run there ain't much time to enjoy the good weather. As I sat with the engine idling, Ashley asked me if I could turn up the stereo so that she could hear her favorite Beyonce song. I melted when I looked at her sitting in her booster seat as she began moving to the rhythm of *Dangerously In Love*. About ten minutes later, Promise rushed in to the car.

"Hurry up and pull off baby!" he instructed sounding kind of nervous.

"Why? What happened?"

"Audrey, just drive! Get on the Cross Island Parkway and head towards the Verrazano Bridge! Hurry up! Go!"

I did as I was told but couldn't help but wonder if Promise had seen a cop or what. I didn't know what to think. Promise reclined his seat all the way back. I could see his chest rapidly rising and falling as he hyperventilated.

"Promise, you ok?"

"Yeah, yeah, I'm good," Promise said as he exhaled very deeply.

As soon as we were back on the Parkway, he let out a

sinister smile as he handed me a bulging white envelope.

"What's that?"

"I think its like five grand. I just got 'em niggas!"

"You just got them niggas? What are you talking about?"

"The bank, I just robbed them."

"Promise, you just robbed the bank?" I asked in a bit of disbelief, shock, and disgust. "Promise, no you did not just rob that damn bank! What the hell!"

"Yes, I did, I just said this is what I am, what I do!"

Promise took the envelope from me and he began to count the money right in front of me without any regard for his daughter who was watching and listening to everything.

"Promise, you serious?"

"Yes, baby! I'm dead ass! This is me! I'm a stick up kid. We gotta skip town and we need this money so we can live. I ain't never had a ATM card or a bank account in my entire life! This is how I do my banking!"

Promise paused and added, "Look! Robbing a bank ain't what I wanna be doing, especially with my daughter in the car wit' me! I'm just doing what I gotta do! Every cop in the city is looking for me, and baby I ain't got too many options right now!"

"But, Promise, I told you I got over $300 on me plus my credit card with me."

"Audrey, listen, I want us to make it to Virginia, the Hampton Roads area. And when we get there, we're gonna need money! I got a daughter, I got you, I got the cops looking for me, and it's not like I can just up and get a job at Home Depot or something!"

I didn't respond to Promise. I just looked straight ahead and I kept my eyes on the road. Reality had just slapped me in the face as I sat there listening to the music blaring out of the speakers. I was rolling with a straight-up thug! I couldn't fathom how he could shoot a cop, kill him at that, and then in a relatively short time thereafter, just walk into a bank as calm as hell and rob the joint!

Okay, the cop-killing thing, I could explain that away and say that it was a reflex thing where he'd just gotten caught up in the heat of the moment. But the bank-robbing thing, I really couldn't get it.

Promise explained how he went to a bank counter and acted like he was filling out a withdrawal slip while in actuality he wrote a note saying he had a gun and instructing the teller to quickly take all of the money in her drawer and put it inside an envelope. Then he got on the line for business banking customers since those tellers held the most money in their drawers and passed the teller the note. In a flash, she handed him the money and he bounced.

After listening to him detail his criminal act, I watched Promise gleefully count his loot and when he was done counting, he spoke up, "$5600, baby! Not bad for five minutes worth of work, right?"

In disbelief and with a somewhat hidden disgust for Promise's flagrant attitude, I reached forward and I changed the radio station. Ironically, 50 Cent's hit song *What Up Gangsta* was on. I looked at Promise and I nodded at him to pretend as if I was in agreement with his suggestion that the $5600 was in deed good pay for five minutes of work.

"Yo, yo, turn that up! Turn that up! Yeah! I love this nigga, Fifty!"

I turned up the music but apparently not loud enough. Promise reached the volume button with his index finger and he turned the music as loud as it would go. As I drove and navigated through a developing parkway traffic jam, I listened as Promise shouted the hook to the song as loud as he could, "What up blood, what up cuz, what up blood, what up *gaaangsterrr*!"

At that moment, it was confirmed that Promise and myself had to have been *wired* different at birth or something! This was his hero and what he aspired to. I shook my head thinking these thoughts. Finally, for my eardrum's sake, the song ended and Promise lowered the volume. With the radio at a decent decibel, Promise continued to amaze me by coming across so detached from the circumstances that we were in.

Promise turned around and looked at Ashley and showed her all of the money that daddy made from his heist. Then he asked, "Does my baby girl wanna go to McDonald's?"

Of course, Ashley agreed. What kid would turn down McDonald's? So Promise ordered me to get off the parkway and to plot a course to the nearest McDonald's so that he could purchase a Happy Meal for his baby girl.

I had successfully driven for four hours. We were traveling south on I-95 and I was sure that we were in the state of Maryland when my mother's cellphone number showed up on the caller ID of my cellphone. I turned down the music so that I would be able to hear what my mother had to say.

"Hey Mom," I said as tried to sound as calm and normal as ever.

"Audrey, where the hell are you at?" My mother screamed uncharacteristically into my ear almost rupturing my eardrum.

Before I could answer, my mother continued on, "I knew that nigga was no good! I knew it! With a name like Promise, I should have never gone against my instincts. That boy ain't nothing but a damn thug! And what kind of name is that anyway? He ain't nothing but a broken promise!"

I looked at Promise and I stretched open my right hand so that my four outstretched fingers could sort of make an opening and closing motion with my thumb. I was trying to indicate to Promise that the person on the other end of the phone was yapping away.

"Who is that?" Promise silently mouthed to me.

"My mother," I silently mouthed back. Promise nodded his head and reclined back in his seat.

"Mom...mom..."

My mother would not let me get in a word without her stepping on my words.

"Audrey, are you with that boy? Answer me, Audrey!"

"Mom, I will answer you but every time that I try to speak you talk right over me. So are you gonna let me speak?"

"Audrey, don't try to get all smart and sassy with me! Not when I come home to a block full of cops and police, and the damn news media saying that my home is suspected of possibly housing a fugitive! Do you know how embarrassing that is? Now, tell me, how do I explain that?"

"Hello...Hello...Mom? Can you hear me? Hello? You're breaking up...Let me call you back."

Although I was faking and acting like the phone had static, I immediately hung up the phone 'cause I didn't wanna hear what else my mother had to say. I knew that eventually I would have to hear her mouth but I felt that she needed at least a day or two to marinate and cool down.

"The cops are at my moms crib," I informed Promise. I made sure not to tell him what my mother had said about him.

"You see that? I'm glad that we left when we did," Promise calmly stated, "The cops, man I tell you," Promise continued on while sitting upright and shaking his head, "They know how to hunt a nigga down when it's one of them that gets taken out but let it have been a nigga from the ghetto who got killed. You think they would care and be following leads the way they doing with me? Hell no!"

My cellphone began to ring again and I quickly turned off the phone. At that point, all kinds of emotions and thoughts were beginning to fill my head as to just what in the hell was I doing. Promise must have sensed the doubt that was starting to get the best of me and he chimed in and took the conversation in the only possible direction that could have taken my mind off of saying, to hell with this whole running from the police ordeal!

"Audrey, something that I don't understand about you is this; When we were talking to your uncle about chopping up the X5 and getting this car that we're in, you mentioned to him something about when your moms died when you were thirteen... But a minute ago, you were just talking to your moms on the phone. So, how could that be if your moms is dead?"

Promise looked at me intently and waited for my answer. Little did he know but he was tapping into one of the major motivators that allowed me to ride with him and his daughter on the ordeal that he was going through.

"I rarely ever talk about this with anyone but when I was

turning twelve years old, my mother was diagnosed with cancer. And it was always just me and my moms for as long as I could remember. I've seen pictures of my pops but I don't remember him. I never got a chance to meet him and talk with him before he died when I was young. Then when she got sick, she and I couldn't do the things that we used to. Emotionally, she couldn't be there for me anymore. That whole year that she battled cancer was the toughest year of my life because I watched my mother live in pain and die a slow death. Before I knew it, she was no longer there."

"I'm sorry, baby, I didn't know," Promise said.

"No, its ok, I mean, I learned to deal with it over time but it was really rough back then. I literally had no family and when I turned thirteen, my moms passed away. One thing led to another and I found myself in a group home and being taken care of by the state. It was the loneliest, most depressing thing that I've ever had to endure. And it came at a time in my life, just before that transition time into my high school years and that was the time that I needed someone to lean on but there was just nobody there for me. It wasn't easy."

"What about your uncle?"

"Well, he had just finished doing like a 25 year bid so he didn't have much to offer me. He was coming outta prison and he was coming home to nothing so what could he do for me? But I thank God for him because I always knew that he was like my ace in the hole that I could count on if things ever got rough or if I ever needed that big-brother protection."

"That is so crazy, Audrey! So if I'm right, it's like you can sort of look at what you went through and project that on to Ashley. And you don't want Ashley to go through the same thing?"

"Exactly Promise! Wasn't it enough that her moms got killed! Poor kid's got no control over these events. So far you've been there for her but if something were to happen to you now she'd end up in a home like I did. Like what happened to me after my mother got cancer and died. Then I was pulled from the only home I'd ever known. Growing up in a group home made me feel cheap and worthless. I can't begin to describe how unwanted and unloved I felt. At the same time, I knew that God is real. Every night I'd pray to him and I asked him to find me a home and find me a new mother and things like that. And so..."

Promise knew where I was going and he finished off my words, "Oh, so you're adopted?"

"Yup. And I don't know if you know all of the emotional baggage and issues that adopted kids and foster kids go through but it is no cakewalk. At age fifteen, I was really fortunate 'cause I was far from being a cute cuddly baby that most families adopt but, against all odds, I was adopted by the woman that you now hear me calling mom."

"That's wild," Promise stated, "I guess that we all have our story and we all have that unpaved road that we had to travel at one time or another."

"You right about that but we gotta make sure that little girl sitting back there doesn't have to travel down no unpaved roads," I said as I turned and glanced at Ashley. She had fallen asleep with her *Happy Meal* toy placed nice and snug underneath her right arm.

We'd finally reached our destination of Hampton, Virginia and we decided to check into a hotel that wasn't too far from Hampton University. Promise and I were both exhausted. Poor little tyke was knocked out and dead to the world. When we reached our room, I plopped myself on one of the two queen size beds and, if I had allowed myself to, I could have fallen fast asleep in under a minute. Promise woke Ashley up so that she could use the bathroom and then he tucked her into bed.

"You hungry?" Promise asked.

"Nah, I'm good. I can wait until the morning to eat. We should go to the Waffle House for breakfast."

"Ahight, we'll do that."

When Promise and I were done with the small talk, we undressed and decided to take a shower together. Not until I was undressed did it hit me that I didn't have a toothbrush, pajamas, slippers, a change of clothes, or even an extra pair of panties for that matter. I spoke my thoughts to Promise and he assured me that we would all go shopping in the morning to get some new gear and purchase some of life's essentials like toothbrushes and deodorant.

While we were in the shower, we both took turns lathering one another up with soap. Despite all of the hectic events that had been transpiring, it hadn't caused Promise to lose his touch. He had hands of gold and as he massaged my back, he caused chills to run up and down my body. I turned around and we both kissed while the water ran down our faces and our bodies. It felt so good to just experience Promise in a sexual and passionate way and I made sure to block out all of the thoughts about him being a cop killer, a bank robber, and a thug.

Those thoughts were easy to block out considering that

Promise soon had his *magic-stick* inside of me and we were making love, doggy-style, right there in the shower. Usually, I'm the loud screaming type when I have sex but knowing Ashley was sleeping in the other room dampened my ecstasy. I tried real hard to control my passionate responses.

We went at if for fifteen minutes and I wanted him to shoot a double feature but at the same time, I knew that we really couldn't enjoy ourselves the way we wanted to so I had to take what I could get when I could get it and not be greedy.

As we dried off our bodies and made it back into the bedroom, I hugged his naked body, kissed him on the lips and said, "Baby, I just wish that we could do nothing but make love all day long."

"Tell me about it," Promise said as he gripped both of my butt checks and scooped me up off the ground.

As he held me up in the air and against his hard chocolate body with his hard dick pressing against my belly, I wrapped both of my legs around him and before kissing me, Promise looked me in my eyes and he assured me by saying, "One day, this on-the-run thing is gonna be behind us. Trust me, it won't be too much longer before we get past all of this. You got my word about that. And when this is all over, I'm gonna go to Jacob The Jeweler and ice that ring finger for you. After that, we're gonna fly to Hawaii and get married on the beach."

I didn't respond. I just held onto him and hoped that his wishful thinking would one day come to pass. The two of us eventually made it into the bed. We didn't even bother to turn on the T.V. as we just laid in the dark and cuddled under the sheets together. I was thinking about saying a silent prayer and then going to sleep but just as I was about to pray, Promise's words interrupted me. While he would eventually sleep like a baby for the rest of the night, it was his words, or his request of me that would keep me awake tossing and turning like a colicky baby until I finally willed myself to sleep for the night.

"Audrey, I know some people who I can hook up with that stay down here near Norfolk State University. And I got a plan that could get us some money and give us some breathing room for a while."

I didn't want to say anything that might burst Promise's bubble but I knew that whatever he was devising, it was something illegal. I kept quiet and let him talk.

"See, some cats from New York moved down here to hustle. I could stake out them cats and rob them but I don't think that would be the right move. If I can get up some money, I can have you travel back to New York, make a purchase for me, and bring back some product and have these cats move it for me."

I surmised that by purchase, Promise meant buying some illegal white powder. I remained silent as I was trying to figure out exactly what to say to him so that he could see the fruitlessness mentality that his lust for crime had trapped him in.

Promise continued, "You seen how easy it was for me to get that money from that bank, right?"

"Um hmm," I said.

"Well, they got a whole lot of ECSB branches down here in Virginia. And the reason that the ECSB branches are a good-target is because none of their branches have bulletproof partitions that separate the bank teller from the customers. So, if they get passed a note they're more likely to go with the demands because they know that they got nothing at all protecting them from getting shot at point blank range."

Hoping that Promise would just hurry up and get to the punch line, I simply added another "Um hmm."

"See, I figure if we hit three more branches and get about twenty thousand between the three then we would be good. I know I could flip that real quick! But, baby, what I need is, I need you to go in and pass the note to the tellers for me."

There was the punch line that I had been waiting for. I spoke up. "Promise, I got your back, and all that, but that ain't the kind of work I'm looking for. Plus, we ain't gotta do that. I can hold us down. I can get a job and take care of us."

Trying his hardest to convince me and sell me on his plot, Promise sat up and reached over to the nightstand and turned on the lamp, which caused both of our eyes to squint.

"Come on, baby, just three notes. That's all you gotta do. Pass three notes for me and we good! I wanna take care of you. I don't want you taking care of me. I just need your help on this! You know I would have no problem doing it, but it's that my mugshot is about to be all over the place in a minute and it would be too risky for me to try anything. But if we hit three branches in the same day, back to back to back, then we'll be good. It won't take more than like three hours, if that! Nothing is gonna go wrong baby. Trust me."

I buried my face in my hands as my heart began to race. And all I could think about was the last thing that my birth mother ever said to me when she taught me this on her deathbed. She read to me and it comes from the Bible in 1 Corinthians 15:33. I could actually see and hear my mother reading those words that say, *"Do not be misled: Bad company corrupts good character."* I heard her voice louder now.

When my mother knew she was leaving this earth, she

told me there would be many things that she wished she could be around to guide me in but being that she was sick and couldn't help where she was going, she told me that I would have to rely on and trust God to guide me so that I would always do the right thing. She made sure though that she stressed to me that even if I trusted God to guide me, at times in life I would be faced with peer pressure type situations and that in those situations I would need to remember the words of scripture so I would not follow the crowd and do wrong simply for the sake of doing what others want me to do, or for the sake of wanting to be accepted by others.

Trying to not get pinned down into making any stupid decisions, I said, "Promise, turn out the light. Let's just both get some sleep and in the morning, we'll talk about this."

"Nah, baby, I just wanna know," Promise said sounding like a spoiled child. "You love me, right?" he asked.

"Promise, don't go there."

"Okay, well then it's done. After we leave the Waffle House in the morning, we'll get ourselves two Nextels and then we'll stop at the mall and get some clothes and all of the other stuff that we need. And when we're there, we'll make sure to buy you three different pairs of shades and three different hats so when you go in to the banks, you'll have three separate looks that won't give away your identity."

I didn't respond to Promise partly because I was tired as hell and partly because I was trying to figure out how, without my consent, had Promise just *volunteered* me to rob banks for him? I was also considering the words from the Bible that my birth mother had spoken on her deathbed. I glanced over at Ashley and just the sight of her influenced me so I sunk my body deeper into the mattress and pulled the covers over my head.

"Go to sleep, Promise," I instructed, "And turn out that light."

Promise did as I said and as he spooned me in the dark, I was trying my hardest to will myself to sleep. He didn't say anything else to me but I could tell that his mind was racing a mile a minute plotting and scheming.

As the three of us sat and ate breakfast at the Waffle House, I commented to Promise how I thought that one of the waitresses looked and sounded a lot like the character, Flo from that hit TV show, *Alice*, from back in the late seventies and early eighties. Flo was the one with the accent that would always yell at her boss Mel and tell him to 'Kiss her grits!'

At first, Promise didn't know what TV show that I was talking about but when it finally hit him, he agreed with me that the waitress in fact did have a striking resemblance to Flo. So, as we sat and ate Promise spoke to the white lady and asked her did anyone ever tell her that she looks like Flo.

"Oh, I get that all the time, baby. If I had a dollar for everyone that told me that I'd be rich."

Promise and I chuckled, while Ashley didn't have a clue as to what was so funny. Little did we know that Promise had just sparked the talkative juices in our waitress - Flo.

"So, where are y'all from? Y'all sound like y'all from New York City," Flo said with a big bright smile as she commented how cute Ashley was.

At that point, Promise and I began to fumble over our words. At the exact same time, I blurted out that *we* were from Long Island and he blurted out that *we* were from Pennsylvania. Flo looked at us with a confused look on her face. I realized that Promise was more than likely trying to protect our identities so I quickly made an attempt to clean up my slip of the tongue.

"We are originally from Long Island but we moved to Allentown, Pennsylvania about five years ago. I guess we just never lost our New York accents."

Flo smiled and said that she could recognize a New York accent in a heartbeat.

"Yeah, I used to live in Brooklyn years ago."

"Really?" I chimed.

"Yeah, I used to live in Coney Island right down the block from the amusement park but that was way back in the late sixties, before you guys were even born."

Under the table, Promise nudged my leg trying to get me to shut the heck up so that the conversation with Flo could end. I took the hint and realized that too much running of the mouth was definitely no good because if Promise's face just happened to show up on TV, or on some wanted posters, or the newspapers then holding conversations with people like Flo would do nothing but help to jar their memory at a later date.

Flo eventually went to serve other customers, which gave us some time to engage in private conversation. From a distance Flo could see we were talking about something private, so aside from asking if could she us get anything else, she kept quiet from there on out.

I was glad that she had left us alone because Promise had begun to talk about me renting an apartment in my name as quickly as possible so we could get up out of that money-draining hotel that we were in. We spoke about that at length and we agreed that in a few days that I would do that, in terms of using my name and my good credit rating to secure us an apartment somewhere in the Newport News neighborhood.

Before long, we made it out of the Waffle House and made our way over to the mall. Promise held true to his word and after buying some toys and candy for Ashley he purchased about five outfits for each of us. He also made sure to purchase the necessary essentials for us like toothpaste and deodorant. Since I had discarded my phone as had Promise, we also purchased two Nextels.

Promise was like most men, in that while I wanted to shop and browse in and out of stores, he wanted to get the hell out as quickly as possible. Not that he was worried about protecting his identity; it was just that he hated, shopping like a 'goddamn woman' as he so eloquently put it.

By about 12 noon, we had made it back to our hotel room. Ashley was so drained from all the running around that she headed straight for bed so she could lay down. Promise proceeded to place his large wad of cash inside of the small safe that was in the closet while I put the new clothes on hangers and inside the dresser drawers. Promise turned on the TV and began to surf channels.

He stopped when he reached CNN Headline News. Both of our mouths dropped as we watched and listened as they reported on the New York City police officer that had been killed. But what really had caught us off guard, and I guess we should have seen it coming, was when they flashed a mug shot of Promise.

"Daddy!" Ashley shouted with joy as she quickly sat up,

smiled and pointed to the TV and shouted, "Daddy's on TV!"

Little did she know that her daddy being on TV was in no way good. Not wanting his daughter to see him on TV in that fashion, Promise quickly turned the channel.

"See, Audrey, that's why I didn't want you running your mouth the way you were with that 'Flo' waitress!"

I couldn't believe Promise had just snapped at me with the tone in which he had used. I wanted to blurt out that he needed to check his short-term memory and realized that it was his slow-ass who had started the conversation with the lady.

"Promise, why you snapping at me?"

"Because you ran your mouth when all you had to do was sit there and eat!"

I knew that Promise was frustrated and agitated because he had just seen his cover blown on national television but I couldn't just sit there and get blamed for something that wasn't my fault.

"Hold up, baby! I know that you're stressed out and all but it was you, not me who started the whole conversation with Flo in the first place. So don't try to put this off on me!"

"Oh, so you're blaming this all on me?"

"Promise, I'm not blaming nothing on you. All I'm saying is that I barely said anything to the woman! You are the one who first spoke up.'"

"What the hell was that 'we're from Long Island'? What the hell was that for?"

"Okay, look. I can see this ain't going anywhere. And what's done is done so if you want me to take the blame then fine, I'll take the blame!"

"What?"

"What do you mean, what?"

"I'm sayin', why are you all of a sudden trying to disrespect my ass?"

"Promise, what are you talking about? Ain't nobody trying to disrespect you. Look, obviously you are just stressed out because of everything that's going on and I understand that so lets just drop the whole thing."

"Nah, I'm not dropping a got damn thing!"

I couldn't believe this whole new side I was seeing of Promise. I guess he's the type that cracks under the pressure. Then I began wondering if my uncle Brandon had intuitively sensed something that I had failed to see as a warning signal.

As Ashley pleaded for her daddy and I to not yell, Promise kept digging deeper, "I'm not dropping nothing! I see your little pattern! First you talk all slick and then you just wanna drop everything!"

"Promise, what in the hell are you talking about me talking 'slick'? Are you trying to call me a snake?"

"Oh, now you're gonna play stupid! No, I'm not calling you a snake! You know exactly what I'm talking about!"

I couldn't believe that this utterly ridiculous argument was taking place.

"No, Promise, I really don't know what you are talking about! So tell me, what are you talking about?"

"Last night, that little stunt that you pulled. I was talking to you and practically pouring my heart out to you and asking you for a favor. And it's like I'm vulnerable right now and you know I need you but your ass chose to ignore me and just go to sleep! In essence, you just wanted to drop the subject just like now you wanna drop it! I'm just waiting for you to drop me! Matter of fact,

I'm not begging your ass for nothing. If you wanna drop me and drop everything, then do that! You can take the car keys, get in the car, and head your ass back to New York right now!"

"Okay, okay... Whoa! Whoa! Wait a minute. Lets just please slow everything down for a minute," I said as I looked at Promise and saw how vexed he was.

"Promise, you're saying that you asked me for a favor, like you'd ask to borrow some milk or something. But that wasn't the kind of favor that you asked of me. You asked me to rob a bank for crying out loud! Three banks at that! Maybe it's just me but that is a whole helluva lot bigger than a favor!"

He remained quiet and he didn't say anything. Promise simply started popping the tags off of some of his new gear and began getting dressed. When he was done getting dressed, he did the same for his daughter.

"Before you head back to New York, can you just do me one more solid and I won't ask you for anything else. It's not the apartment. I'll figure out how to take care of that... All I want you to do is just take Ashley and me to a car rental place and rent a car for us. That's it! You can keep your BMW. I gave your uncle my word that it would be your car and I'm sticking to my word. Plus, by you keeping the car that will be like my payment to you for all you've done for me up to now."

I didn't know if Promise was playing with my head or if he was dead serious but I did know that he was good at manipulating my feelings.

"Promise, I'm not leaving your side."

"Audrey, forget it! Just like you've been saying to me, just drop it. We'll be ahight. I'll get this money up and me and my daughter will be ahight."

Promise was really convincing me that he was in fact serious. I wanted to request that he at least let me take Ashley back to New York with me but I doubted that he would go for that.

All of a sudden, I remember wondering and thinking to myself that Promise really must have been spoiled as a kid or something because he had managed to deflect everything off of himself. He spun things in such a way where he was making me feel guilty for not enabling his ways. He was coming across as if he was the victim or something.

As much as I didn't want to do it and knowing that it would be going against my mother's deathbed advice, I began to put on one of my new outfits. I put on one of the hats that I had purchased along with my shades. Promise looked at me and I know that he had no clue what I was preparing for but he kept quiet.

"Pass me my bag, baby," I instructed, "and hand me the car keys too."

Promise did as I instructed.

"Look, its just about 12:30. We already wasted enough time. Now, if we're gonna hit these three banks before they close at three o'clock then we need to hurry up and let's do this," I said. I could not believe the words that were coming out of my mouth.

Suddenly, like a kid who had been told that he was off of punishment, Promise's whole demeanor sprang to life. He approached me with a huge smile plastered across his face. As he hugged me, he spoke into my ear and said, "Thank you so much baby!"

I shot right back, "Promise, we don't have time for all of this hugging. Lets just hurry up and do this before I change my mind."

"Okay, okay," Promise said as he scrambled around the

room to retrieve my other pairs of shades and my other hats as he prepared for us to depart and do our dirt.

Before departing, Promise did manage to sit me down at the table that was in our room and he had me construct the three separate notes that I would pass to the tellers. He also went over some last minute logistics so that I would know and be clear on just exactly what it was that I needed to do.

When my quick tutorial was over, Promise placed his loaded silver hand gun inside my bag and told me that I wouldn't need to use it but that it would be there at my disposal just in case I had to scare or really threaten 'some clown ass that might try to flex' as he put it.

All three of us quickly left the hotel room. After Ashley was strapped into her booster seat, Promise and I headed towards our first destination. As we drove, we talked and we agreed we would check out of the hotel as soon as we were done hitting the banks. Things would be way too hot to stay there.

As usual, I did the driving so that if the cops stopped us, chances would be that only my driver's license would be checked. And unlike Promise, I didn't have any warrants out for my arrest so with a clean record it made logical sense for me to do all of the driving.

Promise didn't want to use one of our new Nextels so he had me stop at a pay phone so he could call information. He got the number to ECSB customer service and called to get the addresses to the branches located in the Hampton Road area.

"There's a branch near the Coliseum Mall that's not too far from here," Promise said as he got back in the car.

At that point my heart was racing so fast and my palms were so sweaty that I couldn't think straight. I barely understood or heard Promise as he was instructing me how to get to the mall.

"Audrey, you ok?"

"Yeah, I'm good. I'm just nervous as hell"

"Don't worry. It's gonna be easy. Just pass the note to the teller, that's all. It'll be just like passing her a withdrawal slip," Promise re-explained in an attempt to ease my fears.

"I'll be ok. It's just that in my wildest dreams, I never ever thought that I would be doing something like this! Word!"

We reached the parking lot of the Coliseum Mall and thankfully, the bank was not actually inside the main part of the mall itself. The bank stood alone about a good one hundred yards or so from the mall. Rather than walk the hundred yards, I navigated through the parked cars until I reached the bank.

"You ready?" Promise asked as I pulled into a parking space behind the bank.

"Yeah, I'm ready."

I didn't say another word as I mentally prepped myself to go through with this bold criminal act that could easily land my ass in a federal prison if I were to get caught.

Ashley broke my concentration as she spoke up and asked, "Ms. Audrey, can I come with you inside the bank? Please."

"No, sweetie," I responded, "Just sit here with your daddy, I'll be right back."

I exited. The walk to the bank felt like it took forever! My legs felt like a ton of bricks. My mouth was as dry as an Arizona desert. My palms were so sweaty I was afraid that I might smudge the ink on the note that I had to pass to the teller.

When I entered I noticed everything and everyone. It seemed as if all eyes were on my black ass. I slowly made my way over to a counter and pretended as if I was filling out a deposit slip. Although it was just in my head, I really felt like everyone was watching me, customers and all, and that intensified my extreme anxiety.

Since it was Friday afternoon, the bank was overcrowded but thank God – if I can say his name in a situation like this – that the line for business customers only had one person standing in line at the time.

I got behind the only business customer and he was soon called. My heart began to pound so I knew that it was now or never. Audrey, just turn around and get your black ass up out of this bank! Girl, you're crazy! What are you doing in here? I kept questioning myself. You ain't no bank robber! The response was felt and I couldn't think clearly.

The customer ahead of me was taking way too long. They must've known something was up, what I was preparing to do. Maybe they had already signaled for the cops to come and were trying to stall me until they came. All those thoughts ran through my head and the teller finally greeted me pleasantly, "Hello, you can step forward."

With my powder blue Roc-a-wear sweat suit on and my S. Carter sneakers, I stepped forward. My dark shades hid my eyes in a mysterious kind of way but with the hat that I was wearing, it allowed the shades to naturally flow with everything and I simply looked like some hip-hop chick. The only thing that was out of place was my Burberry bag because it didn't match my outfit at all but that was a very small and minor detail.

The teller looked so much like Britney Spears it was amazing! Somehow, even though my mouth was now drier than an eighty-year-old vagina, I managed to genuinely smile. I don't know where I mustered up the smile but it drained a lot of tension from my body.

The Britney Spears looking teller smiled and asked, "How can I help you?"

Hoping that I didn't show my nervousness, I exhaled and I tried to run game as best I could. "I know people must tell you all the time you look like Britney Spears," I said to the teller as I reached my hand inside the Burberry bag and gripped the gun.

"I get that all the time," the teller acknowledged.

"Take it as a compliment. I mean, after all, Britney is a pretty girl." I don't know why on earth I had said that because I didn't want that chick to think that I was hitting on her.

"Oh, thank you for the compliment," she gleefully replied.

I was thinking that the small talk was over and it was time to hand her the note and I did just that. I made sure that I also placed the Burberry bag onto the counter top and I kept my right hand inside the bag. The gun was literally pointed at the teller and my finger was on the trigger.

Britney, as I like to call her, read the note.

This is not a game! The handbag that you see on the counter has a loaded gun and it is pointed directly at your head! Place a large quantity of large bills inside an envelope for me and pass me the envelope. Don't panic and don't look alarmed and don't alert anyone and no one will get hurt.

After reading the note, "Britney" looked up at me with a "deer in the headlights" look. I simply gave her an uppity, sophisticated diva smile and commented under my breath. "This ain't a game! Hurry up!"

My heart was pounding. As nervous as I was, I could now see and understand how Promise had pulled the trigger and shot that cop in the heat of the moment because, at that present moment in time, I was so scared my nerves could cause me to accidentally pull the trigger and pop the teller for no reason.

Britney did as the note instructed and handed me a letter size envelope stuffed with cash. I looked inside real quick and confirmed that there were large bills inside. Without saying thank you I turned quickly around and walked out of the bank. I wanted to run but didn't want to bring more attention to myself. I was so nervous that I couldn't even breathe until I got to the car.

When I got to the car, the engine was running. I opened the driver's door and handed the money to Promise. I finally took a deep breath. Dramatically exhaling, I said, "Promise, that was the scariest thing that I ever did in my life!"

"But you did it, baby! Yes! That's what I talking about! That's my girl right there!"

It felt good to hear Promise cheering me on but I was more concerned about how to quickly navigate out of that parking lot. Promise directed me and we were quickly off to our next spot.

While we drove, Promise wanted to know all of the details of what had transpired inside the bank but my nerves were on edge and I wasn't in the frame of mind to talk. I just wanted to hurry up and get the other two robberies over with.

The second ECSB branch was about two or three miles away and we reached it in no time. It was located on a relatively busy boulevard called Mercury Boulevard.

"Promise, don't take my silence as disrespect or anything

but I just wanna stay in my zone until we get this over with."

Promise understood. As I put on a lighter shade pair of sunglasses and a different color hat, Promise suggested that I take off the top half of the sleeveless sweat suit that I was wearing. Even though we had just hit the other bank, he didn't want to take the chance that a description of what I had been wearing had already been broadcast to the other banks in the area.

His suggestion was good and it proved my theory that in crime situations, there is always one calm person that can think logically and that person is usually not the perpetrator of the crime, the one with the adrenaline flowing rapidly throughout their body.

So after taking heed to Promise's suggestion, I took off the sweat suit top and walked into the second bank. I was wearing a white tube top and since my breasts are so large, the tube top couldn't contain those two bad boys. My nipples were protruding through the tube top like two huge Del Monte raisins, not to mention my cleavage was showing for days!

Since I had just hit the other bank, I couldn't waste anytime fiddling around inside. I headed straight for the teller lines, not stopping to pretend to fill out a deposit slip or anything like that. Ironically, the line for business customers was quite long and the line for regular customers was short. I took a calculated chance and just got on the line for regular customers.

The reason that I say calculated is because it looked as if the white male teller was ready to call the next customer and I was desperately hoping that he would take me first before calling one of the business customers to his regular line to be helped. My calculated move paid off and the late twenty something white male signaled for me to come to his line.

Everyone knows that white guys love themselves some

big titties in the same way that black guys love big butts. I had purposely wanted to get this white boy teller because I wanted to use my protruding boobs to try and distract him.

When I reached his station, I made sure that I relaxed my handbag and my entire right arm on the counter so that the bottom of the handbag was facing the teller. And I also made sure that I visibly rested my titties right there practically spilling out on to the counter, as if I was serving them up on a platter or something. The white guy smiled and couldn't help but look at my chest.

"So, how are you doing today?" I asked. I wanted the white guy to think that I was flirting with him.

"I'm doing fine and yourself?" He said, his blue eyes glued to my chest.

"Not bad but I'm kind of in a hurry."

"Okay, how can I help you?"

"Well, I wanna make a withdrawal," I said passing him the note.

Before he finished reading, I spoke up under my breath in an attempt to speed things up.

"Baby, this is not a joke so hurry up!" I said as I removed my titties from the counter top so he would no longer be distracted. I kept my hand on the trigger inside my handbag, which still rested on the counter top, pointed at the teller.

In record time, the teller had complied with my demands and handed me a stuffed envelope. I didn't look inside. I said "thank you" as I turned and made my way outside back to the waiting vehicle.

Unlike the previous parking lot, Mercury Boulevard was the perfect boulevard for a get away because in a matter of seconds, I was driving and in the mix with the rest of the other cars. As

I pulled off, I exhaled and I handed the envelope full of loot to Promise.

"That was actually easier that time," I informed Promise.

"It's all down hill baby after the first one," Promise explained with a huge sparkling smile plastered across his face.

Promise directed me towards our third and final bank location. As we drove, I was in more of a mood to talk. Sounding very animated, I stated, "Baby, that last one was so funny! I had to go with my gut instincts and I didn't get on the business line. I just got on the regular line because the business line was more crowded. So there was this white teller. He looked like he was about twenty-seven or twenty-eight years old. I walked up to his station and propped my titties on the counter along with my handbag and it was so funny; he was drooling over me! That was probably the closest that he ever came to some dark meat in his life. So, while I had him drooling, I slipped him the note and he didn't know what to think. So, I was like 'baby, this is not joke so just hurry up!' Yo, homeboy handed me that money so quick! Oh, it was so funny 'cause his blue eyes was so wide open and I know he couldn't believe that he was getting got the way he was!"

Promise laughed and he commented how I was real smooth with mine. Then he told me that he had counted the loot from the first bank and that there was a little over eight grand in the envelope.

"Eight grand?" I asked in astonishment.

"Yup."

"Damn, I guess crime does pay," I joked.

Promise and I both began laughing. We were quickly approaching the last branch and Promise stated, "Okay Audrey, this is the last one. Just do exactly like you did on the other two.

Get in and out as fast as you can. Remember the third time is always the charm so relax and stay calm."

When I reached the last branch that was located not too far from Rip Rack Road, on a street called Settler's Landing, near Hampton University, I told Promise that I thought I needed to completely remove the hat and the shades just in case all of the banks were hip to my M.O.

"Nah, keep on the shades. Don't worry about the hat but what you do is this, here, wear my t-shirt," Promise said as he began taking off his shirt. "It'll look over-sized on you but that's ahight cuz it's a completely different color. You had on all light colors before and now this shirt is black so you should be good."

I took Promise's t-shirt and put it on over my tube top while Promise sat in the car with his wife beater on. Just in case, if someone had seen us leaving one of the previous banks, we decided to park in a gas station that was right near the third bank. The last thing we wanted was the cops or anyone else catching us out there because of the car that we were in.

I have to admit I was contemplating not going forward with the third robbery. After all, Promise had damn near five thousand dollars in the closet safe back at the hotel. I had taken more than eight grand from the first bank that I hit. So right there was thirteen grand that we had accumulated and we hadn't even counted the money from the second bank!

In my heart, I just felt that we didn't have to risk hitting the last bank but I was afraid to speak up because we were on such a roll and so far, there had been no hitches in the plan that Promise had devised. There was really no need to start doubting him. But, in all honesty, I was also thinking that maybe Promise should hit the last bank simply because if all of the banks were hip to me by now then they would more than likely have all of their employees on the lookout for a suspicious looking black female, not a black male.

We were in the gas station parking lot and my heart began to rapidly pump gallons of nervous blood through my body. I never spoke up about the reservations I had. I figured that hitting this last bank was like taking medicine and I need not complain. I just needed to do what I had to do and get it over with.

Something didn't feel right and I could tell that Promise also had some doubts about our chances of success on the last bank. I say that because as I was stepping out of the car, Promise said, "Yo, if anything don't look right on my end I'll get in the driver's seat and I'll key you on the Nextel but I won't say anything. So, if you hear the chirp coming from your Nextel, that means that sump'n is up and I want you to get your ass back to the car as fast as you can with or without the loot. Okay?"

"Okay," I said, closing the door and fearfully made my way inside.

When I entered the third bank, things just seemed eerie and surreal, as if things were moving in slow motion. I scanned the bank and noticed that this bank was the most crowded of the three that I had entered.

I made my way to the counter in order to fake like I was filling out a withdrawal slip and that's when I noticed that there was a security guard standing near one of the teller locations.

Audrey, get your ass up out of this bank right now! They know what's up. I kept saying to myself. I didn't hesitate and I quickly made my way back to the car.

"That was quick," Promise noted.

"They had a security guard standing right near one of the tellers! Things just don't seem right, Promise."

"Don't sweat that, baby. All banks usually have a security guard or something. But I guarantee you that he wasn't holding no heat! He ain't nothing but a toy-cop, an unarmed security guard."

"I don't know, Promise."

"Come on, baby, get it over with. Matter of fact, I'll tell you what. Give me the note and I'll just add on the note that the teller better not alarm the security guard."

I shook my head and thought about things for a couple of minutes. Then upon reflection, I decided to go along with everything. I exited the car and made my way back inside. My heart was beating so fast that I thought it was gonna jump out of my shirt. By the time that I had made it back inside the security guard had re-positioned himself and he was now standing near the doors.

I blocked everything out as I stood on the long commercial line. While waiting, I thought about how good it would feel to go home and sleep in my own bed, to just relax and end all the drama I was putting myself through. I thought about these things so that I wouldn't psych myself out of going through with the robbery.

Audrey, when this is over, we're checking out of that hotel. You are renting an apartment for Promise and then you are taking your ass back to New York! No more of this gangster's girl nonsense! I told myself. If anything, I'll just make a pact with Promise that if something ever happens to him, I will do whatever it is that I have to do to get custody of his daughter. I'll be there for him in that way but I can't ride with him any longer in the manner in which I'm riding with him.

Finally, after about fifteen minutes of waiting, I reached the teller. The teller was a middle aged white lady and the moment that she saw me, I could sense that she probably had been alerted to lookout for someone who fit my description. I say that because both of her eyes immediately shifted to the right side of her head and she began acting fidgety and nervous. Most likely, she was probably thinking back to a description she had given her of me, the New York bred Hampton Roads bank robber.

Without speaking any words of hello or anything like that, I passed the teller the note. I put my handbag on the counter with my hand inside the bag and my finger on the gun's trigger.

"I know that they probably told you to be on the lookout for me. And I know that you know who I am. So just play everything cool and calm and do what the note says."

The lady read the note and immediately her face went pale and she looked flustered as if she had just seen a ghost.

"Oh my God. Oh my God! This is not happening. I can not believe this is happening!" She said.

Under my breath, I spoke in the sternest tone that I could muster up, with my teeth clinched tightly together, I said, "Lady, if you do what the note says I will not hurt you! You gotta do this quick 'cause I don't have all day!"

Little did the teller know that I was probably more scared than she was. I quickly darted my eyes off of her and glanced to see what the security guard was doing and he was looking right in my direction. Fortunately for me, the teller was carrying out the demands of the note as the guard suspiciously looked on.

"Just one more second, please just give me one more second," the teller begged.

"Stop talking and hurry up!" I barked with my teeth still clinched together.

As the teller handed me the envelope, I noticed one of the other tellers looking closely at what was going on. She had to have tripped some alarm or something, I told myself referring to the nosy teller that had suddenly begun to scope things out a bit too closely.

I knew that I had to move very rapidly and get out. There had been nothing smooth about the third robbery and I wanted to make it back to the hotel so we could talk calmly. I planned to tell Promise my mission had been accomplished and that I would be heading back to New York. This would definitely be the end of the crime road for me.

As I prepared to walk past the security guard, I tightly gripped the envelope full of cash and my handbag both with my left hand. Out of force of habit, if I am walking to my car, I always reach for my car keys before I actually get to the car. So due to my nervousness as well as force of habit, I began searching in my pocket for the car keys. Totally forgetting that the car keys were still in the car, I began to panic because I was thinking that I had misplaced the keys.

I frantically reached into my pocket a second time and that's when I remembered that the keys were still in the car's ignition. Realizing that I had made it past the security guard, I blew out some air from my lungs. As I reached to push open the door that led outside the bank.

The security guard spoke up and said to me, "Um excuse me..."

Not knowing what to do, I stopped dead in my tracks but did not turn around to look at him.

"Goddamn! I'm busted!" I whispered to myself. "Just go, Audrey, just go!" I urged myself but I was literally paralyzed with fear and remained still.

Then the security guard sounded as if he was heading in my direction and he began to speak again only this time more assertively, "Excuse me Ms.! I think you dropped..."

As the security guard was in the middle of his sentence, my paralysis suddenly left me and I reached my hand inside of the hand bag and grabbed the gun and, without thinking, I spun and pulled the trigger all in one motion.

I caught the unarmed security guard with a hot one right in his stomach. The sound of the bullet discharging from the gun was tremendous! The security guard fell to the ground writhing and screaming in pain as something fell out of his hand. At that point, all hell broke loose as people inside the bank began yelling and screaming and ducking for cover.

I turned back around and violently pushed open the bank doors, trying to get the hell out of Dodge as quick as I could. In the process, I knocked down a customer on his way in. Sprinting like a track star, I made it to the BMW, and jumped in the driver's seat screaming hysterically.

"Oh my God! Promise! Promise! I shot the security guard!" I screamed literally trembling with fear.

"What happened?" he asked.

"I don't know! I panicked and I turned and shot the security guard without thinking! He called out to me!"

As I continued to just shake with fear, Promise yelled at me to forget about what had happened and for me to hit the gas pedal and drive.

"Drive!" He screamed as sirens screamed all around coming from every direction.

I didn't know where I was going as I weaved my way on to a different road. I saw cops speeding by me as they apparently were making their way to the ECSB branch I had just hit. Before I knew what was what, I realized that I was on I-64 and somewhat in the clear.

My intention to stay quiet until we reached the hotel broke loose. "Promise, I can't do this anymore! I gotta get back to New York!"

"Okay, baby. I understand. Just get back to the hotel and we'll check out and sort everything out then," Promise said as he attempted to calm my fears.

"No, baby. You don't understand me. I just have to leave now! I can't wait around and help you get an apartment or anything like that down here. I just gotta go! The cops are after me now! I can't believe this!"

Promise tried his best to calm my fears and he told me that he would more than likely troop back with me to New York and try to get in touch with Squeeze and Show and hole up in the Bronx somewhere.

While he spoke, Promise convinced me to make one last stop back at the hotel. There were about five thousand reasons for him to desperately wanna stop back at the hotel so I didn't go against his wishes. But I wanted to just get out of Virginia, get on I-95 and head north, like yesterday!

With my heart still pounding and my nerves ready to explode, I said, "Promise, be in and out! Don't go to the checkout desk or nothing. Just get the money out of the safe, grab those clothes, and lets get up outta here!"

Promise agreed. We pulled into the parking lot of the hotel and he quickly jumped out of the car and headed to our room.

"Ms. Audrey, what's the matter?" Ashley innocently asked.

"Nothing, baby. I was just scared about something, sweetie," I said to her trying my best to come across as if I was in control. "Don't worry, everything is gonna be ok. We'll get you some McDonald's real soon. Okay, sweetie?"

"Ok," Ashley replied.

At that point, I closed my eyes for five seconds and tried to relax. With my eyes closed, I replayed the scene of me shooting the security guard. Then all of a sudden it hit me like a ton of brick! I realized what had happened inside the bank was that when I was exiting. Searching for my car keys, I must've dropped the credit card looking for the hotel room.

"Ugh!" I said to myself in anguish as I realized that my hotel room key had simply fallen out of my pocket when I had been frantically searching for the car keys and the security guard was only trying to alert me I had dropped something. Audrey! How could you have been so stupid and panicked like that? When the guard had said 'Excuse me, Ms. I think you dropped...' he was just trying to help. "Damn!"

I opened my eyes and checked my pockets and sure enough, it was gone. After checking all my pockets, I noticed four unmarked cars parked outside the hotel. They looked like unmarked law enforcement vehicles. Two of the cars were empty but the other two were not and four white men quickly piled out.

"That's the police!" I hissed myself. They must have found the hotel key the security guard had and they traced it back to this hotel! Ah man!

I reached for my Nextel and used the walkie-talkie feature and I urgently said, "Promise, forget the money! I really messed us up! We gotta leave right now! Hurry up and come back to the car! Now! Hurry up!"

Promise hit me back and he sounded like he was running and out of breath or something as he yelled into his Nextel, "Baby, take Ashley and just go. Don't wait for me, just go!"

"Promise!" I yelled into the Nextel.

Promise came back on the Nextel and as he was yelling for me to leave him and to just go and drive off without him, I could hear someone in the background shouting.

"FBI, don't move!"

I started up the car and peeled off in reverse. Promise chimed back in on the Nextel, "Audrey!" he yelled and I heard a gun shot sound come through on the Nextel.

"Oh God!" I said fearing the worst.

I put the car in drive and peeled off. Suddenly the car filled up with this red misty looking substance as if someone was spraying some type of aerosol red spray paint into the car. Before I knew what was up, I couldn't see a thing and everything inside the car was red. I later learned the last bank teller had slipped a dye-pack into the envelope along with the cash.

The dye-pack, like most dye-packs was on a timer and it got tripped when I walked out of the bank with the stolen money, the same way a store alarm is tripped if you were to try to walk away with stolen merchandise. Once the alarm was tripped, it activated a fifteen-minute timer that released the dye and stained the money and my clothes, Ashley's clothes, and the entire tan leather interior of the BMW. The dye-pack had done its job so that the money had become useless to us because it was now very recognizable marked money.

The next thing that I remember after the car filled up with red mist was that I crashed into something. I don't know what it was that I had crashed into because I couldn't see where I was going. Then I remember all four of the car doors being violently ripped open. I was suddenly yanked out of the car and rammed to the concrete pavement. I heard the sound of men and women yelling, "FBI, stay on the ground!"

I knew at that point, a big chunk of my life if not my entire life was over but my thoughts were still with Ashley.

"There's a baby in the car!" I yelled.

"Shut the hell up!" One of the officers said as he jammed his size thirteen foot on the back of my head and neck area. They were frisking me.

As my face lay on the concrete, I was thinking about how painful the officer's boot was as it pressed on the back of my neck and prevented me from breathing. I attempted to turn my head so that I could get a small bit of air into my lungs but in the process, all I managed to do was rip and tear the skin off the left side of my face as it scraped against the concrete. It was so bad that the white meat was showing.

My arms were then jerked and yanked behind me and twisted up like a chicken wing. At that point, I heard someone yell, "I got the baby!"

I wanted desperately to look and see what was going on with Ashley but I couldn't move. The officers and agents had put the cuffs so tight, it felt like the cuffs had broken both my wrists.

"Get up!" One of the FBI agents yelled as they continued to manhandle me and yanked me up off the concrete.

They escorted me to an unmarked car. As I walked with the oversized T-Shirt stained with red-dye, my face scraped, bleeding, and cut up, my wrists were numb and stinging. I couldn't help but think over and over about the Biblical words that my mother said from her deathbed.

"Do not be misled: Bad company corrupts good character."

Too bad I didn't realize the truth of this statement until the end.

ANTHONY WHYTE

I was running as hard as I could, dodging and ducking bullets all the way. These people in front of me better get the fuck outta my way. Running so hard, I could feel my heart pounding about to bust outta my chest. Breath coming in serious gasps, and sweat beads pouring down my face, blocking my vision. I couldn't see them but knew I didn't shake them. One more block, with angry pursuers dogging my tracks. Got to keep it moving and look for a way to exit this hood alive.

Dipping left, I dodged, hid and viewed the entire scene. It reminded me of childhood and being chased by bullies through the playground. I didn't want to spaz but I couldn't help but think there was nothing else to do. Just when I ducked down and thought I'd outrun them, the goons on foot spotted me. I had to move faster and get the fuck up out or these niggas will bury me.

Hardly any traffic on the streets this early, so I ran in search of the entrance to the subway. I wasn't a punk. I was just trying to make a clean getaway. Not caring, my body crashed into dope fiends as I ran. Early morning and I'm knocking down ladies of the evening as I skipped across the quiet boulevard. Along with the fiends, broads wearing next to nothing were the only ones out this morning.

"Where's the subway station?" I slowed and asked one of them, breathing hard.

"Couple a blocks over."

The response was barely off someone's lips when suddenly there was a bright flash of headlights. I heard the tires screeching then boom, boom, boom, gunshots exploding. I jumped over a baby carriage pushed by another fiend trying to figure if it was cannons they were shooting.

Almost out of breath, I hit the blacktop running, trying to

get the fuck up out of Bushwick. I made it past the bodega on the street corner. The only light I could see was the red and green glow from lamps next to the subway station.

After a few blocks, I slowed a little and dipped down the stairs of the station. Suddenly I realized how close on my heels they were to me. I stumbled and went rolling down the urine soaked stairs of the New Lots Ave subway line. Crawling on hands and knees trying to recover.

All I heard was: Backa! Backa! Backa!

I stayed low dodging three shots that rang above the roar of the train. I felt the burn on my insides and smelt my flesh afire. Bullets crashed through to the bones under my clothes leaving my left thigh numb for a couple seconds. Everything became blurry as intense pain surged to my brain.

Angry voices of threats hollowed as if I was trapped inside a time warp machine where sounds doubled, as movement slowed. Sweating hard and accelerating but only managing to move at a snail's crawl. This had to be the repercussions of robbing Nine and his crew.

My lungs burned from grueling inhalations. I was determined not to die out here in these parts where no one knew my rep. I had to make it. Call my boys. My homies, where were they? I didn't wanna die. I ain't really lived yet, I kept telling myself.

My breathing was labored and I could barely run but continued to struggle. Every move I made felt too painful to endure and the bullet holes burned like hell. Sluggishly knowing that my luck was running out, I dragged on.

"Yeah asshole, what you got to say now? Huh, huh what? Huh? What you gon' do now? This is what you get for robbing my girl, you bi-yotch!"

I heard the yelling and straining my neck I tried to peek at them. These cats chasing me weren't Nine and his crew like I'd thought.

"Yeah, fight like a man, coward. What, you too scared to fight a real man, huh? You ain't scared to rob a girl?"

This threat was from another set trying to off me for jooksing some broad. That's it? They hunting me for robbing a broad? What broad?

For a moment, the thought swirled in my mind yet I couldn't remember. From behind a pile of subway trash, I could see three of them. They were all Spanish with mugs that showed no mercy. These clowns have got to be loco. This had to be some kinda crazy mix-up. I mean getting killed over a broad, these cats got to be fuhgazy!

"Man what girl I rob? I ain't robbed no broads!" I yelled, thinking I could buy time.

As the words rolled off my tongue, the answer immediately struck me like a bullet to the head. I'd given up my position and they took aim with the answer.

"The bitch you robbed a couple weeks ago, cock-sucker, that's my sister. No one messes with my sis - You fuck with my family - you die, muthafucka!"

The rats began to stir and the noise caused a welcome distraction. I thought carefully for a minute while their backs were turned. They could call me pussy, I wasn't gonna show out. I'd live to fight another day. The question of heart reared up. Was I scared to die? There was a definite struggle between acting brave and dying a coward. At the same time, my heart was telling me to turn around and fight to the end. I gave it a thought and zing!

Bullets coming closer than I expected jumpstarted my efforts to escape.

Gun clapping around me sounded like fireworks on the Fourth of July. These cats weren't afraid to let lead fly. I had no other choice but to run. It was the best thing I could do in this situation. I mean I'm gangsta and would rather be busting back at them but these three here walking toward me, plus the one who was driving the car, meant that it had to be about four of them. I gripped my nine-millimeter tightly. There was only one thing wrong: I had an empty clip but my mind was amped with wishful thinking.

"Ya'll fuckin' kill me and it's all-out war! Y'all be dead. So why don't we just put da guns down and talk about this deal."

"My guns speak for me puta! Die! Die maricon!"

"Y'all ain't see nuthin till my peeps come huntin' for y'all."

I yelled then sat, completely out of breath feeling my chest heaving as they drew closer and closer. I could hear the yelling and name calling accompanied by a staccato of rapid gunfire.

I kept out of sight thinking of what I could do against these niggas coming hard-body. I peeked out as rounds flew at me. Another man fired twice and the bullets ricocheted inches from me. It was now or never, I had to make a move.

"Go to fucking hell, moron. Tell Satan we sent ya!"

Guns blasted. I covered up, dodged and ducked. The voices grew thunderous. For a second all I heard was the echoing going on in my brain. It scrambled my senses, making it difficult for me to think.

"Y'all fucking around! My dogs will hunt y'all to the grave. Ya heard me?"

"Who's fucking gonna hunt me, puta?"

"Tell 'em sons-o-bitches to come get at Carlos. Round here, I'm da fucking man!"

"Show that faggot no mercy! Shoot him! Make him bleed! Make him cry!"

Guns continued blazing. I bounded from the trash heap after the firing ceased and could hear the voices. I jumped down on the train tracks and stayed frozen, nervously waiting until they weren't looking my way then I could skip out. I listened diligently as the voices got closer.

"Where's that little pussy at?"

"Come out and play little putty…"

"He over here, somewhere. Come out you lil' faggot boy!"

They were clowning me. I heard their taunts and whistles, the rustling of their footsteps getting closer. Off in the distance, I could hear the train whistling toward the station. Now I definitely had to make a move or the oncoming train might crush me. I jumped back onto the platform and as soon as I did, the gunfire resumed.

"Don't let him get away. Wet that nigga up!"

Again, another outburst of rapid fire came at my head. I ducked down, no more time for thinking and planning. I had no choice but to react and the only action was to run faster than they could. I'd chosen this life of crime with the realization that anytime my demise could come.

Gangsters supposed to die young. Here I was on the brink of living, struggling to hold on. I sucked up the pain, limping and dragging my leg. Couple blasts went off and I was reminded of their anger. It came through loud and clear.

I felt a sudden pain tearing my insides apart and realized that I was bleeding like a stuck hog. In my efforts to get away in the worse way possible, I limped some then hopped and ran as hard as my injured leg would allow.

Huffing and puffing, I ran as best I could. I didn't want to go down without a fight but felt pain searing through my back and thigh. I thought I'd lost them when suddenly I heard voices fuming mad.

"There he is!"

"Get him don't let him escape!" They yelled, trying to catch me.

Bobbing and weaving, I fought my way through throngs of passengers standing on the platform grimacing after seeing my blood stained clothes. Some shrieked hysterically and pointed with horrified looks on their faces as I struggled past them. Blood squirted from holes in my chest. I became woozy from the bleeding. The white wife-beater I was wearing was now crimson red.

I was determined not to let them catch up but was I really running out of time? I suddenly lost balance, tumbled while attempting to limp to the token-booth. My bloody appearance made a big statement causing a wave of panic on the platform.

The clerk saw me coming, took one good look, and I witnessed deadly fright written over her face. It wasn't supposed to end like this, was my last thought before the frightened clerk yelled.

"Ohmigosh! Call the police!" She screamed.

I saw her collapse. The train was held in the station and minutes later, I sensed po-po swarming. They surrounded me and attempted to take a statement but I was too tired to give them one. The cold seeped in as my blood flowed freely on the concrete. I tried to focus but my eyes rolled uncontrollably as the paramedics started working on my bullet-ridden body.

"The gunshot wounds look serious," one of the paramedics shouted.

"We gotta be quicker or we're gonna lose him," another said.

His fists held instruments and I remembered him pumping hard against my chest. I was drained and weak, I could barely keep my eyes open. I knew I had to. My life depended on me doing so.

Seconds away from death, the paramedics took their time in carting me off on a gurney heading to Kings County Hospital. For them this was another routine stop in a life of crime I had chosen. Some people say the situation makes the person. Going on this journey, bullet holes leaking blood from my body was par for the course. I chose this lifestyle and what came of it was unavoidable.

The siren wailed loudly as the ambulance sped through miles of road. Meanwhile, I was seconds from being another fatal sad statistic on the landscape of urban American reality.

Madukes warned me about it coming to an end. Getting snuffed somewhere caught off guard faraway, in a place like this. I could hear her voice ringing loudly warning me, "All mobsters eventually get locked away for life or get carted out leaving their loved ones to mourn 'em. None ever, ever walk away."

The ol' earth told me going down this road would be a life sentence. She had been wrong before. It's ending this way because I wanted to be gangsta. No one was there to save me. Everyone was too busy judging me.

Above the wailing siren, my mind was playing tricks. I could still hear madukes' mouth. All the time she be bitching and griping about everything from welfare check-to-welfare check.

"You're gonna be nothing but a common thug. You can't keep robbing people everyday. Someone's gonna kill ya eventually."

My life coming up was filled with her complaints about one thing or the next. I had to take it to the streets of New York trying to get nigga-rich.

"Why don't they give me mo' money? I can't survive on pennies. They know I got two chil'ren and things expensive," Madukes whined all the time. Whenever I'd be stupid enough to agree, she'd let me have it.

"Yeah ma, you right. I think they should give us mo' money," I'd say, "The government ain't trying to let us live, they want us barely surviving..."

She never let me finish. Madukes refueled on some Gin and juice, and be ready to jump down my throat.

"Since you agree, why don't you go out and get yourself a real job instead of sittin' there like a damn bookworm writin' nursery rhymes?"

She'd put me on full blast and ridiculed me one too many times in front of my younger sister, Lindsay. My mother, Ms. Donna Parrister, never offered teaching, only criticism. She had a mouth on her that kept going loud and strong and annoyingly all day long. Without any real proof, my mother made the claim we were descendants of Blackfoot Indians.

Madukes said the story goes like this. One sunny afternoon way back when Jesus was a still a baby, some white men captured and raped her great-great-great grandmother. That was the reason we shared the family heirloom: hazel eyes. The gene ran through a family I had never met, not even once. We called city housing our home and lived there all our lives. No relatives ever came to visit. I wore my inheritance well though. These hazel eyes of mine got me plenty attention from the broads. My mother, who had something to say about everything, never let anything go unsaid.

"You just can't get everything on good looks alone." She offered when girls started calling me on the regular at home. "Pooh, why you got these hood rats calling my phone every minute? I will put a lock on this phone because you're not paying any bills up in here."

"What's up, ma?" I'd ask when I could no longer ignore her.

"You wanna know what's up?" She'd start and then the sermon would go nonstop. "You need to go out and bring in some money every now and then, that's what's up. If you ain't gonna go to school, you'd best go get yourself a job so you can have some damn money and stop depending on me. I'm not gonna be living up in here supporting your lazy ass. Blah, blah, blah..."

I wasn't really hearing her. I'd sit there concentrating on poetry lines and tune her out until she threw criticism at my poems.

"You just sitting there at the table like some lil' bitch writin' damn rhymes. Why don't you go out an' do sump'n." Or her favorite line, "You ain't neva gonna 'mount to nuthing." At which point she'd realize I wasn't paying her attention and she'd turn to my sister. "Lindsay, pass da 'mote, girl, and don't be like your brother. He's just another lazy ass," she'd laugh as she channel-surfed.

A sure sign that madukes didn't know what the fuck she was talking about. Plus she was a high school dropout and as I grew up, I proved her wrong. There was never unity in the family at home so I was destined to find one on the outside, in the streets of Brooklyn.

The ambulance made its way through the hectic streets, stalled at times, only by early morning traffic. I felt life slowly easing on and the realization that I'd never live to see the sunlight again weighted me down.

I hadn't just lived life, I thugged street-life. Me and my peeps took it over with heart, gloves, masks and guns blazing anytime. My eyes were tearing as I squinted uncontrollably. I'm dying alone but my peeps will be there like always.

In the beginning we were inseparable, down for each other. There was Squeeze, Promise, Show, and the baby of the bunch, me, Pooh. We put a stranglehold on hustlenomics with so much force in the streets of New York that chedda, cars, hos', and clothes came in a huge smash.

From day one, they were tight with me. Older fellas but they always looked out for the kid. I enjoyed hanging with them and eventually we became a notorious crew. After awhile it seemed that my street fam was all I had.

We dreamt of being filthy rich. And we each wanted to control a sector of the crack industry. While they hustled, I was young'n, the lookout who would steer customers to my crew, telling lies to keep jakes off them.

Next stop, I understudied in hand to hand, for a small take until I graduated all in and became full partner. We financed big drug deals with the Dominicans. Loot from all that nigga-money became Mickey Mouse game to me. Ever since I was a lil' shorty back in Brownsville, I hustled hand-over-fist to make major Jewish money.

Growing up poor and knowing my family could barely make it, made me hunger for much more. It was so bad sometimes that we'd recycle gifts at Christmas. My sister and I were too young at the time to really care but at school when classmates got mad at us, we got ragged-on.

"Whose turn is it to get the fruitcake in your family?"

Kids teased us at school. We were clowned until we'd both missed many schooldays. Life was hard but we were young and having fun living it but the guidance counselor said I had "anger issues which lead to my behavioral problems." I enjoyed escaping to my world of poetry.

After being picked on a couple times by classmates, I stopped showing my poems and stuck around until the 6th grade. I had to leave because I was getting into fights on a daily. But dropping out did not quench my thirst. I kept on composing poetry.

This was the softer side of me that teachers and family knew but I kept it hidden from the rest of society. I didn't want that side of me exposed cuz where I'm from that'd make you look cream puff. And you didn't want soft on your resume.

I came up rough and tough in a place where you scrambled for everything you wanted. The wild side of a Brooklyn housing section known as Roosevelt houses was a place called Do or Die that I'd made my rest. You could call it my home. My peeps and me made out like bandits. They taught me that big bank always take little bank. Our only worry was planning how much money we wanted to stack. We were ripping and robbing drug dealers and their clients. We figured if we could supply the supplier then we'd be the number one suppliers. The crew set up biz along Fulton and Throop.

There will be those who will question why I chose this life of crime. I'll be the first to tell you there are no regrets. It was about wanting not to be broke but it was also about the love of balling and the rep it gave me one the streets. As a shorty on the come up, seeing my family as poor as could be, I didn't want to keep repeating the cycle. I didn't want to be on the sidelines. I wanted to ball.

Being born poor is like a disease you inherit. The only way to survive it is to make a lot of money. Getting paid was my motivation, that's why I hung with the big boys watching the hustle, knowing that one day I'd be on. I grew up with pain and I wanted to have all the riches that having chedda could bring.

I started learning my lessons in hustlenomics, doing my thing on the streets. I wanted the baddest broads, the fastest cars. I learned from jump, if you play your cards right, everything you need was here; all that money, power and respect.

The ol' heads taught me that when niggas know how you got down dirty for ya cheddar, they'd give you respect. It was that, straight up. They told me that the road to the riches wasn't laced with sands of gold but with bullet holes and long prison terms. And once you committed, once you walked down that crooked road, there was no turning back. The street was like a jealous lover.

Out here, you couldn't love nothing but the freedom to do you because everything that you fell in love with, the streets would take right back. Whether it was broads, clothes, family, friends, pussy, money, a new BM, and that big guardu. The streets giveth and taketh. No questions asked.

Your other love was the protection you carry inside your waistband. Whether it's a four-five or nina, the heat enhances your chances to survive the streets. Ol' heads' are big on respect. Respect your set or crew. And keep everything you do between you and the crew.

No matter what, never become a snitch. That's signing your suicide note. On the streets, they may drink and laugh with you but in the end, nobody gives a fuck about friends. Killing you to protect their dough was just a part of the way cash flowed.

Me? I was always on the hunt for the next broad and then the next broad to replace my ex. I constantly lay traps for the next broad to place on my dick-list. Man, if I tell you once I'll say it twice. I roamed. It was my only weakness. Whichever broad I'd catch, my head would be on her pillow to the next morn then I was out. I did the deed then on to the grind with my peeps.

My nigs and I would hang out all day long, thugging ghettonomics. At nights out on these streets, we would watch the crack fiends resurface like roaches. We'd catch them trying to get their breath and sell them more rocks cut from our freshest stock. They'd be starving for the base hunting and making promises to pay like they'd have the money the next day. But we already knew there'd be no tomorrow.

"Pay now," we'd say, "we don't want know brains or coochie...money talks..." That was the motto.

Getting brains for a piece of rock was a common thing. Fiends are greedy and very early we saw the potential for tremendous growth in the crack industry. Squeeze had an idea to rob from the big timers and sell to the street hustlers for a nice price. They would peddle the drugs on the streets and be hooked to our prices. Around the hood, we supplied the suppliers. Quickly the dealers became our number one customer but they were also targets.

After doing a day's dirt at the Do or Die, I'd creep back late nights to Brownsville where I held down a crash-pad I'd rented after moving out madukes' apartment. There, I slept sedated by the heavy sounds of my neighbors' sexual lullabies. Then, like clockwork, the loud barking of gunshots would wake me.

This was the late nineties. Our set riffed and tussled, handling our biz like bullies in a playpen, we were executing our grind on the streets of New York. I was down forever with the cats I hung with on a regular.

Promise, he became the older brother I didn't want, always trying to steer me out of harm's way. In the beginning I looked up to him then my dude started bugging with baby momma drama.

Squeeze was the gangsta all the other niggas imitated. Every team needed a live one like him. He had heart. I witnessed Squeeze bust this cat straight in the face for saying some dumb shit like calling his girl ugly. Squeeze did have some ugly broads for real though but if you ain't know him you couldn't say shit to him 'bout it. Whenever that nig was dissed it would be all out war. I rolled with him so I should know or you could ask my other man, Show.

Show, always tell you the truth cuz he don't give a fuck. He's a big ass black ugly mug for a- Matter fact, Show, big and ugly enough for three people, maybe four. It didn't matter though because he was a college bound all-star football player. Back in the days, the pretty broads would cling to him like static to wool due to that one fact. Show had prettier broads than everyone else around 'cept for the kid, you dig?

So many bitches, so little time. I can't even begin to name them all. I remember when it all started. See, I was blessed with the fucking cute hazel eyes that made bitches go wild. I'd hit a blunt or smoke some o' that bomb-bomb zee with a bitch and my eyes would get to changing colors, ooh-wee. Lovemaking would be off the hinges.

Whenever I stared in a broad's eyes, I could see them fantasizing about wanting to fuck me. All I had to do was snap my fingers and panties would drop. Bitches love a handsome thug and that's what I was. They'd glance at me and if they looked more than once, it was over. At a party I'd get tapped on the shoulder and the dopest broad would be waiting to dance with me.

"Hi, I don't know if you've noticed but I've been here waiting for you to dance with me…"

The prettiest sump'n in the spot would be on me like that. My niggas stayed mad cause I'd steady pulled their little girlfriends. Bring your girl 'round me and if she looked in my eyes, it was on. Her panties be wet like she at the beach on a hot summer day. Pretty soon she coming up outta them bikinis.

Every night since I was about thirteen, if not grindin' I'd be beatin' up some buns. The kid was blessed, ya heard me? I can still see them even now creamin', watching my eyes go from fiery red to green and all the shades between. The colors would go from green to brown to blue to purple, anything a broad wanted to see. Just stare into my hazel eyes and that fire would start traveling down below her navel. My name should be on a star like those on Hollywood Boulevard.

No apologies, I had a bunch a broads and I was living large. Seven nights a week, different pairs of legs be trembling and pussy wet you already know. I'm getting in a zone and jumping ahead of myself.

Everyday we used to meet at Squeeze's pad in the basement where his uncle stayed. Squeeze would kick his spiel. Then we'd move out later in the evenings to do our dirt, hit niggas up and break out as usual. It was a simple job. No need for sweating.

Squeeze liked to sell that shit for bargain prices to some people he knew out in South Jersey. Me, I preferred going further down south to places like B'More and all that dark country metro area, down south to D-ware and all them parts.

I remembered once we'd gotten about thirty pounds of weed off these cats out in Philly and then we called Squeeze's peeps out in B'More. They couldn't pay cash so they told us about their man in Virginia who could sponsor the weight. We spoke to him on the phone and he invited us down to VA.

On an early summer night, we met a pimp named Harry, at an upscale nightclub. He was a fool and thought that because we partied with him and his girls, we wouldn't rob him. Maybe it was the baby blue '72 Cadillac we rolled up in. That weekend was Show's birthday. He bought the whip and had it tricked out.

Harry loved the way the ride looked and made several offers for the whip. He liked our style and the way we handled our BI. We were rocking crushed linen Armani suits. It was either the champagne or the way we conducted ourselves put Harry's head in a spin.

The risk had already been calculated. We were on the job and were gonna bag his dumb ass for some big cash. Except in the process, I also caught my first body.

We met him while mobbing up in the club. Harry was a big man, tan with a mid-east accent and a love for Moet. Like gentlemen we splurged a little on Show's birthday weekend. Squeeze was always running his mouth about biz, talking loudly and getting us all kinds of attention, some unwanted but mostly wanted. Harry, who claimed he was; the man, sat at our table and enjoyed our celebration.

Quickly we gathered info about his entire stable of mules. They were running on Peter Pans back and forth, north to south, east to west. His girls were charming and they doubled as his only security.

"What crazy fool would wanna hurt any of these beautiful women?" Harry threw out as he spoke glowingly of his stable.

He traveled light except for his girls. They were strapped with Luis Vuitton and cute pearl handled pistols. The pimp had done time and hated violence of any type. Six broads made up his security team.

Man that just didn't make sense when you were in the type of biz we were in. The more we found out about Harry, the more it was confirmed that he would be the next vic.

I listened to the chatter then got bored when the conversation turned into another Squeeze sting. He would make crazy claims of what we were holding, mostly lies. Then the mark would boast of what they've got. Eventually Squeeze would decide if the cat was fat enough for us to bag. I liked Harry's girls and danced off with two. Later, Squeeze met us by the dimly lit bar.

"Excuse me ladies, bidness before pleasure," I said dismissing the two broads with pats on both their protruding buns. Promise and Show joined us.

"Besides Harry loving all that Mo, what else did you find out about him?"

"That nigga do drink a lot of champagne, dogs," Squeeze chuckled.

"Word up. When you left, we ordered like four more bottles and half went down his fucking throat."

"He claimed that 'round here they call him the H-Man cause he be sitting on stacks o' cheddar."

"Let's fuck his bitches," Show said. "That'll be a good weekend."

"Nah, we could do that later, son," Squeeze started. "This mu'fucka wants us to go back to the telly with him and guess what?"

"What, what?" Show shouted as if he was holding the winning ticket in a lottery drawing. We all looked at him. Squeeze continued to talk about robbing this fool and I focused on bagging a couple of his broads.

Harry's mules were scheduled to arrive about three-thirty in the morning. They were coming from the bus depot. This nigga was so impressed with our sale that he was trying to get us to buy some keys off him. He thought we were da legit bidness type. We were but we really weren't. We sold the fool twenty pounds of quality 'dro we'd lifted off some other fools in Newark at gunpoint.

Normally, that grade of weed could run you anywhere from three to four-grand a pound. He was buying it and paying cash for it, on delivery, we gave him all twenty for fifty-grand. Real bargain for us considering we ain't spent nothing but gas and tolls. I don't know what Squeeze told him about us, but the cat was so impressed by our way of doing business, he wanted us to see just how major his operation really was.

About three in the morn, we left the club and rode a few

miles to the Day's Inn. Harry had a couple adjoining rooms. Music and champagne flowed free. We had to wait around to collect our fifty-grand anyway.

Harry enjoyed listening to DMX. The music blasted as we partied up with his six girls. Squeeze, Show, and I all had our man-hoods glazed by these broads. Even though we were celebrating Show's birthday, Promise was fronting like he wasn't feeling too good. Time passed and we were getting edgy waiting for the dough so we could bounce. It was getting closer to that time when the mules would come. We were carefully monitoring H-Man when he approached us with another offer.

"Listen guys, down here in VA things do move slower than up north where y'all from. Because it's taking longer than I expected to get all of the cash and I know you've been patient with me, I've got a deal. How you say it? I've got a fat ass deal for you."

"Okay, okay," Squeeze said and all our ears perked.

"I've got a major shipment coming through. Y'all could stick around and take some back up to Boston with you," Harry said with a smile.

Promise looked shook and started giving off worried signals with his face but Harry continued, "You gave me a very nice price on that smoke. I'd surely like to return the favor." He was wearing a smile that was either deceiving or devious. "It's taking too long to come up with that fifty-thousand, so here's what I'm thinking of doing. I'll give you twenty-five thousand cash and your other half in some good white powder," he said to our surprise.

We were thinking, and rightly so, that Harry was coming up short money or either putting us on the waiting game. This fool was offering us both drugs and money. Now to four thugs outta Brooklyn, that was a damn good offer. How could we turn it down? Now all we had to do was rob Harry the pimp of his drugs and cash. Did he really trust us like that?

"We gotta discuss this amongst us," Promise said acting a little petro.

After sitting down next to a mini bar, Promise said nothing but winked to the camera. This could be a set up. Maybe Harry's plan was not to let us leave the State for Lovers with his dough. We knew what had to be done and shook our heads. Finally, Squeeze whispered below his breath, "Let's take the whole deal, dogs."

"I got *a* bad feeling..." Promise started but Squeeze had already decided. It was his call and for the first time I saw a tinge of yellow really seeping from the mouth of Promise.

"Let's do the deal," Squeeze said. He looked around in each of our eyes. "They're lot of ways we could do this but if the coke is good, let's take it."

"You're saying what I'm thinking Squeeze?" Show asked acting new.

"Yeah nigga, sump'n wrong with your brain?" Squeeze answered immediately.

"I mean, we could get that and take that back and make some more money on top of it," I said.

"We can't be dealin' coke in certain hoods, you know?" Show said in doubt.

"Fuck that. Ain't nobody telling me where I can or cannot hustle in my hood, dogs," Squeeze said getting testy.

"Ahight, so we wid it then?"

Everyone laid hands like we were a varsity team ready to execute the next big play. It was like that, the dirty game we were playing where our guns made us most valuable players. We partied some more until the doorbell rang, and these three fine broads strolled in. It was time for the fun to really begin.

They appeared to be your average sexy looking broads with the bodies of dancers. One look and you could immediately tell that they were carrying heavy weights. Once we identified who *we* were, all we had to do was get into position.

They were very easy preys and we'd already scripted the play. Looking at all these women around the room made me think this Harry fella was getting his pimpin on. I hoped we had no problems cause I'd hate to catch a body I was thinking, glancing at the layout. If any of these broads try something crazy, suddenly I started feeling nervous as the time for execution came close.

The hotel room was abuzz with activity. Six scantily clothed broads wearing only bras and panties were sprawled on a huge bed, chilling. One other broad was there somewhere. Our attention turned to the two mules in the other room with Harry. We had discussed the situation just in case we had to make a fast escape. Promise had volunteered to get the car. He was about to make his move when Harry walked back into the room smiling.

"Here is your twenty-five thousand dollars," he said moving slowly.

I walked to the bathroom as planned and opened the door. It was routine robbery except we knew we were being recorded and that meant we couldn't leave without the video. I sat on the stool and took the weapon off safe. Careful not to drop the gun in the toilet bowl, I slipped the silencer on it. I began to walk out then turned back to flush the toilet.

As soon as I opened the door, I was to blast him if Harry did anything sudden. The door opened and I held the nine on them waiting to do exactly that. Everyone standing either ducked or was running and screaming. In that chaos, Squeeze, whose eyes had been following the drugs, made his move through the door.

"What the fuck are you doing? You're gonna have the cops all over this place in seconds," Harry shouted.

I kept the gun on him while we waited until Squeeze came out with the coke. My hand sweated a little when Squeeze took too long. The gun felt heavier in my hand and I gripped the 9 mm tighter. I pulled the twenty-two out of my boot just in case. Meantime, Promise had ducked out and rushed downstairs to the parking lot.

Bitch-ass didn't wanna be in the line of fire so he went to secure the car. Instead I was thinking that nigga wanted to live to care for his daughter, ducking out when things start popping off. I was built for this. I waited several gut wrenching minutes. It seemed like half hour but I had to make sure my nigga Squeeze was good.

All the time, Harry was cursing and screaming, "I thought you guys were businessmen. You're no businessmen. You're common thugs."

I yoked Harry and walked him to the bedroom door. He opened it and we saw Squeeze with his face up in the broad's ass looking like he was eating her out.

"Ah muthafucka, you got to get your fucking sex on this moment?" Show asked.

"Nigga, I'm trying to get all the coke out this bitch," Squeeze said turning around for couple of seconds then back to the task at hand, removing the coke from the broad's coochie.

"We can work all this out. I've got millions..."

"Shush, Harry, you just tell me where the video is and I'll let your punk ass live," I said and he pointed to the camera.

Show popped his middle finger at it and grabbed the camera. In a flash, we'd be out. We walked out of the room, Harry was still pleading with Squeeze about the big error he'd made.

"You guys can still profit from this business. We don't have to rip each other off. I'm a good man. Understand, I'll forgive y'all for this."

"Really, we don't need your forgiveness," Squeeze said.

And...blam, blam, one of the mules fired a shot from behind. The room was filled with smoke and I turned to see Harry fall then I saw the mule held the 45 in her hand. I was seconds from filling this crazed broad with holes but I noticed she only fired hitting Harry in his back. He never knew who plugged him.

"Y'all muthafucking New Yaak niggas ain't leaving with all the profits," she said aiming the gun side to side, trying to cover all of us. We did not calculate this bit. I was ready to break this broad off some lead when Squeeze spoke up.

"Ahight, so what you gonna do. Shoot all of us?"

"I ain't saying I wanna kill any of y'all. It's that bitch-ass Harry I couldn't stand. I wanna make a deal."

"What you talking 'bout?" Show asked.

"I figured we took a lot of risk and we ain't getting no penny so I'm thinking y'all niggas could hit me with some dough and we'll be straight."

She was still holding the forty-five. I could have blasted her but Squeeze got mushy on me.

"I respect your gangsta but I can't give you what ain't mine, shorty," he said.

"I got kids to feed. This drug money was gonna go along

way, you could split some o' your share," she proposed.

"You trying to rob me, bitch?" Squeeze asked as his cellphone rang. I figured it was Promise probably wondering what was keeping us here so long. Squeeze handed the phone to Show. I was right; it was Promise. Show turned away under the watchful glance of the freak with a gun in her hand.

"This bitch up here tryin..." he started then the broad started getting other ideas. Maybe she thought we were sweet in our Armani suits, sipping champagne and carrying guns because we wannabes. But she opened her mouth and I knew shit was fixing to get all out nasty. I knew somebody was gonna die and it wasn't gonna be from my side.

"Put the phone down," she yelled and my finger that had been itching for the longest minute suddenly reacted and the gun blasted the broad back down. She fell like a sack of bloody mess while the other broads who were crouching everywhere squealed loudly.

"We out, dogs," Squeeze said as another broad fired a shot barely missing me.

"Eat lead, bitch," I yelled as the nine went off in my hand. Her body jerked hard she sprawled on top of the desk. I turned and pointed the nine at the others. They sucked in their breath and fell silent.

We rushed out the door leaving the carnage. Harry was laid out making the carpet red and the two broads were bloody in another room. The other scantily clad broads were trying to get their clothes on as I slammed the door and raced downstairs to the parking lot.

"Let's move, dogs!" Squeeze shouted. We hopped into the car and peeled out, heading to highway 95 N.

"What da fuck was the problems wid y'all niggas? Y'all taking ya sweet time fucking with 'em bitches I bet. While I'm down here trying to figure what da fuck done happened?" Promise was sounding like he was shook.

He looked at Squeeze who'd sat up front then at me and Show in the back through the rearview. No one answered until Show pulled out all the money and coke along with some of the weed we'd sold earlier to Harry.

"We had a small problem," I stated in a matter-fact tone.

"Word? I was down here gettin' kinda worried. I thought y'all up there running trains on 'em bitches and all that bullshit…" Promise started to speak but was cut off by Squeeze.

"Them bitches played themselves, dogs," Squeeze said.

Promise took his eyes off the road for couple seconds and turned around to glance at all the money and drugs. His frown, bitching up his face when he realized how much blood had been spilled for the dough.

"Y'all had to body some…" he began but I jumped in.

"Yeah nigga. I had to shoot them two bitches. They pulled out guns, dogs, and blam!" I said, my index finger squeezing off an imaginary gun.

Squeeze and I chuckled when Show fell against the car seat as if he'd caught a bad one. I began to laugh but Promise couldn't see the humor.

"Blam, blam," Show shouted then mocking the broads with a high-pitched tone he started, "Oh, you shot me, fool. You shot me. I was jest tryin' to rob you."

Show was only living up to his name. He used to be a high school football player who would dance from the knowledge of ruining some quarterback's career with a devastating hit. Now he was laughing at the way those broads died. I guess his impulse was to make light of bad situations. Promise was not feeling us. He screamed at me.

"You young ass fucking crazy fool, you knew the nigga had a camera. Your gun's gonna get us all put away. I'm a tell y'all right here, I ain't living in no jail, dogs."

"Stop worrying so much, dogs," I said to him then looked at Show and asked, "You got the tape right, Show?"

Everyone but Promise knew that Show had the videotape. I wanted to see the reaction from Promise once he found that the tape was secured. I knew that that mug was gonna still be dwelling on it.

"See nigga. Now you ain't gotta worry bout shit else, ahight?" Show stripped the film from the tape. "Here, Promise you can hold this. We even got you a camera too," he laughed. Promise glanced at him with a scowl.

"Ha, ha very funny, huh Show? It don't matter. I'm saying y'all going da fuck overboard." Promise looked around for support but we all knew it was either the broads or us. "Goin' state to state collecting these bodies' gonna make us too fuckin' hot," he said.

"Too fuckin' hot is what we want, nig," I said.

"Oh word, that's what you want huh?" Promise asked.

"I'm sayin' dogs, we family and if I see someone raise a gun, I have no choice but to shoot to kill cuz that's fam," I said.

"Yeah nigga, them bitches was trying to blam me and Show, dogs. The bitch done shot her pimp and then she was fixing to rob us. You feel me?" Squeeze asked giving me a pound. "That gave Pooh here no choice, she had to die."

"All I'm saying is; we've got to slow down with the gun play."

"Nigga, I'm the one taking the burden. That was my finger on the trigger of my mo'fuckin gun sprayin' bitches. Why is your ass actin' petro? You ain't done shit and I ain't gonna ask *you* to hold da weight, done."

"Done..." Promise voice trailed off when Show offered support for me.

"That's real, young un. You da one who left da place ugly," Show said and kept dumping the bag of the bounty in the back seat of the caddy.

Four nice size bags of coke, about a kilo, fell on the redone suede leather of the car. We were still strapped with the twenty pounds of weed and about twenty-five thousand dollars cash. Going through a McDonald's drive-thru allowed us time to ponder the possibilities over cheeseburgers, cokes and fries.

We sat around in the parking lot. Show grabbed a bag of white powder and examined it carefully before putting some on his lips. Then he licked it off with his tongue. He swirled it around like an expert wine taster.

"Shits da real fucking thing, dogs, some pure shit," Show continued dipping and sniffing. "Hmm...not bad, not bad," he said stuffing his nostrils with white powder. His face flushed. This was Show's happy birthday weekend. I was one body heavier, that nigga was one year older.

"Happy birthday, big Show," I said sniffing some coke.

We laughed because he was on the money. This cocaine was the shit. We could tap dance on this and still come off huge. Wanting in on the action, Squeeze turned around looking amp.

"Yeah, what you think about that, huh, niggas?" We glad-handed and Squeezed rolled sump'n sticky.

I could tell Squeeze was hyped; he couldn't contain himself.

Promise was withdrawn and trying to see the bright side.

"I'm ahight, I'm ahight," he repeated between bites of a burger, but through the strain we all could all see he looked strained and was keeping something hidden deep inside. Promise lapsed, forgetting that we had known him a long time. We were like a family.

His face revealed the story his heart couldn't share. Try as he might; Promise wasn't himself at all. He stared straight ahead, remaining tight-lipped all the way. The only person who sat up front cheesing was Squeeze. It was as though Promise had already moved on.

"Ah shit!" Show exclaimed, "This da best fucking birthday a nigga ever had. Y'all my dogs. Yo, Promise don't be scared to pump the volume on my shit, nig," he yelled and clapped his hands when the music serenaded him.

Squeeze got on the phone and in a few minutes, was on the line with a major player up in Greenwich. He agreed to get some of the cocaine off our hands. We gave him a good price as he would send the courier before the end of the day with cash. Things were bubbling.

Although dumping the drugs was going to be easy, everyone's motivation rapidly declined. A few onions remained out of the haul for us niggas to steam when we chilled out. Nothing more.

No one in the clique was a real drug head. We were all recreational users and businessmen. After returning to BK from our VA trip, I could see the changes taking place in Promise.

On the days that we'd hustle, he came through less and less. Squeeze would come up with ideas and dough making schemes that had made us hood-rich and hustlers above all other sets. Although we'd only been plying our trade over a short period of time on this Brooklyn landscape we'd earned the label, Notorious, like Biggie Smalls.

Still we had slowed down a lot. There was time for about a week where the four of us were not together. This hadn't happen in awhile but ever since the VA caper, niggas seemed like they were falling back. I had thought this was what we wanted, all this dough from our gangster-ism. One day as we sat in the basement, in between tokes of a blunt, I voiced my opinion.

"Y'all niggas acting like y'all just don't know. Once you got the streets watchin', you got to live up to that rep cuz niggas gonna see you slippin'."

"Who say we slippin'?"

"Word up man, I'm saying word on the streets is that we slippin. You know things get shysty when niggas start thinking that way. Mugs be thinking it's the best time to hit a nig. Yo, I be out there grindin'. I hear em jackas."

"Yeah? That's what's being kicked around out there? That's what you hear? All I got to say is; me personally, I ain't slippin. Niggas imagine that and I'll lay a mu'fucka out. You feel me?" Show was getting up and waving his tool around.

Squeeze watched Show then said, "Yo be careful you don't fuck up my television, aight."

"Pass the dro, nigga," Promise said. He inhaled heavy and blew a cloud smoke on the rest of us.

"Easy nigga, you stressed?" Squeeze asked but Promise didn't answer and kept puffing.

"Niggas step to me and I'm not gonna hesitate to smack a nigga down. I don't care; I'll catch a case..." Show was saying when I cut him off.

"Man, stop talking all that going to jail shit."

"I'm sayin', dogs. I'll blow a nigga away like you blew them bitches away down in VA. With this automatic shit, I'll what... niggas betta not run up to me looking tough."

"Show, stop kicking all that bullshit. Uncle Junior? Where that nigga at? Uncle Junior!" Squeezed yelled until finally his uncle walked quickly in the living room. "What you doing back there? I hope you ain't smoking up any coke back there, Uncle Junior. I swear if I find that you stealing any coke from back there..."

"Why you call me to come at me like that? I was in the toilet."

"In the toilet doing what?"

"Taking care of my biz. What do you want Squeeze?"

"Lemme find out that you smoking any coke in my damn bathroom. I swear they gonna have to surgically remove these Tims from outta your muthafucking asshole."

"You wanna throw out threats, nigga?"

"Ahight, I'm just sayin. Twist up 'bout four blunts."

Promise raised his hand, choking for a few minutes. "I'm good, dogs."

"That just means more blunts for us niggas," Squeeze said with his wry smile. "Gotcha on that, my nigga," he said pointing at Promise. They both laughed and anyone could sense the camaraderie but at a closer glance, there was evidence of strain on Promise's face.

"It ain't about killing anyone, it's about making that money, man," Squeeze said handing his uncle the weed he needed to roll. He also gave him five dollars.

"Go to the store and bring me back a pack o'Dutchmasters."

"Oh, so that was the reason for you hollerin' out my name."

"Just go on and hurry back, man. I ain't got time for your ol' ass. I got bidness to handle right now, you hearin' me?" Squeeze dismissed his uncle. He waited till he had walked out the room before continuing.

"Look, when all this 'yes' shit stops, niggas will be surprised when we hit them. It's all-good to fall back and regroup. Ain't none of us starving," Promise said. No one was convinced. We had been hanging together since I was in first grade. We knew Promise like we were sure there was something he wasn't telling us.

"I gotta say dat I agree. It's about the money but we gotta wait for niggas to fuck up, then we hit them," Squeeze said.

"Yeah, but the last time we did anything was three weeks ago. What're y'all waitin' for, gold watches?" I asked.

"Nigga please, we got fat while a lot of other muthafuckas starved. Let 'em have their run. Maybe we should fall back for a hot minute and..." Promise said and I immediately interrupted.

"Why? When we come back out, niggas ain't gonna respect us like they did..."

"C'mon man, you bullshittin', Pooh. See you too young to un'erstand that everything takes time...you got dough, a nice fast car and..." Show started but I was too hot to listen.

"Man, I want that bigger dough. That Jew money, nig. This shit we talkin' bout right here, that's chump change."

"You can't be comparing yourself to another nigga..." Promise began saying.

Our voices trailed off when the door opened and Uncle Junior walked in. He scurried pass us to the kitchen.

"Go roll that inside the bedroom, Uncle Junior," Squeeze ordered.

"First, I had to go the store then you're gonna tell me where I should go to roll your weed? C'mon get real."

"If you don't get your bitch-ass da fuck outta here right now, I'm gonna…"

"Keep your shirt on, nigga. I'll go to the bedroom and roll," Uncle Junior said carefully scraping up all of the weed and walking out. "Yeah I better go. Y'all look very heated. Who done bone whose girl? What's done's done," Uncle Junior said in passing.

"Get da fuck out Uncle! Ain't nobody got time for your tired bitch ass questions," Squeeze said. We waited for Uncle Junior to rush out before continuing.

"Y'all know we holding down a lil' bit of cheddar. So it's all good for us to fall back sump'n."

"Yeah but the other side about that is the streets see that all 'laying low' as weakness."

"Listen young un, I agree wid these niggas," Show said and pointed to Promise and Squeeze.

"We know what we holding, but if we fall back the streets might just take that for weakness and we wind up being victims…" I began to say but Squeeze raised his hand and started speaking.

"Right now I ain't saying a crew can't come at us but we gotta be real. It ain't like before dog, we got shit to lose," Squeeze said and waved his hand around. Uncle Junior walked in with four blunts. "Good looking out, Uncle. Them shits rolled like you hanging wid the dread lock brothas on Fulton." Squeeze laughed and quickly sparked one.

He threw a blunt to each of us like when we were shorties and robbed the candy stores in the hood. We had been through a lot but this was like breaking up. All we need is niggas to start singing *Kum-by-ya.* Squeeze offered a light. Promise took a blunt but never lit it. I grew up admiring that nigga. Now he had gone from hard to cream puff.

I puffed on the blunt thinking that our gangsta clique was about to break down. As further proof these niggas had gotten comfortable like the older niggas we had seen growing up, the conversation quickly changed to a discussion about broads.

"Yo, there's a bitch in 2A, I saw that bitch in da club last week Friday…"

"Yeah, she's got a dope body. What's her name?"

"Promise, I know that honey got some friends, hook a nigga up…"

We all puffed knowing that there was no way back to where we used to be. Promise and Squeeze wanted to fall back. Fuck that we had to keep this going. We had that saying, 'We number one'. How we gonna fall back? It's like if a bully stop fighting, the lack of action could give weak ones the heart to come at you. Then it'll be gunning in the streets.

"Lets move out of state, set up sump'n new. NC…" I started to suggest but was quickly chopped down.

"Nah, I'm thinking we lay low. I mean sure if money comes this way then we work that. Promise is right. We could still live well. Do sump'n in couple months…" Squeeze said before Show threw his two-cents in.

"Man, I got a baby on the way…" he said with the big grin.

"My daughter is important, everyone knows this for sure. I'll be the first to let y'all know I'll be damned if I ever fuck her life up," Promise said meeting my eyes directly from across the room.

"I gotta give her a chance, my niggas. I ain't trying to diss no one," he continued looking my way. I was furious.

"Y'all are acting like bitches. Straight up, I ain't never knew there'd come a day when I'd have to say that. That's my word. The way y'all acting right now, I don't know? All I'm sayin' is yo, I'd check if y'all wearing skirts..."

"Man, fuck you!" Show shouted. He jumped and I eased my waistband exposing the nine milli. Show yielded to caution. "What you gonna shoot me like you did that bitch in VA. Pooh? Well you better not miss cuz..."

"That's what y'all wanna do, fight? Pull your gun out? Young un, I'm talking to you," Squeeze said looking dead in my grill.

"Wha' what? I just ain't gonna let any mu'fucka intimidate my ass. I'm gonna shoot his ass if I have to," I said suddenly comprehending the reality; if I had to I'd pull the trigger. These nigs I started out with were growing into some big pussies.

"I ain't trying to get locked up shot up or ruin my daughter's life," Promise said.

"I ain't got nowhere else to go. All or nut'n. This it for me. Ain't no turning back," I said puffing hard on the blunt.

Squeeze left the room and returned a few moments later carrying enough bottles of Moet to go around. It felt like a final date or sump'n. It definitely was breaking up.

We drank and toasted, hugged and laughed at each other's most ridiculous moments. Show drinking from one bottle, and we were using another as an ashtray. Since both bottles were dark, the nigga got so drunk that without warning, he picked up the bottle being used as the ashtray and drank every single roach in it. We died laughing. We hugged and were feeling liberated by the weed and the alcohol.

It never dawned on us that maybe this was the last time we would all sit, and let loose. It was the turning point, the beginning of the end of us. The kids who started it all were no longer motivated. For whatever reason, we all had gotten too old or maybe just too scared to continue. I guess I wanted more. I was lost in my thoughts when I heard the conversation Promise was kicking.

"I ain't trying to get no larger in this. Right now life's good but there's more to living than this...I don't wanna have to kill anyone." I half listened.

"But 'em things bound to happen when you taking over," I said but Promise had made up his mind.

"Yeah, but killin's gonna lead to more killin's. I don't wanna be running around killing niggas, scared the police gonna shoot me or niggas gonna kill my daughter."

The words sounded foreign in the room filled with thugs. Everyone including Squeeze quaked from the boots on his feet to the air he breathed. None of us thought Promise would ever bring it up. The room went silent. Even the loud sound of the TV seemed to go suddenly mute.

Nobody had to utter a word. It was clear that Promise was waving goodbye to the streets and to us, his clique, his buddies down like south for whatever. The whole time I was thinking of my mother and my sister, Lindsay.

I used to hear my mother nag the fuck out of her lovers. Over the years, I saw that nagging only lead to one thing. It always preceded a break-up. Just before the nigga walked out on mommy, she set the tone by cooking a great dinner. Later they'd moan loudly, not caring if Lindsay or I heard them.

The morning after that final big argument, she would know it. She would hope that the nigga would call or come back. No matter how pretty one was sitting, no one wanted to return home from a hard day to constant nagging. The important thing was what would happen the night before, the last date.

No matter how hard we tried, we all knew this was the end. Getting that money, man, had been our motivating chant. Now they had become too fat. They just wanted to sit around taking care of their new responsibilities and enjoying what they'd already made. I had given up everything to be down with them. Was I the Herb, a loser, a sucker?

Sitting here drinking, and puffing, a chilling cold froze my brain. Suddenly I was overcome with a devastating feeling, it would be the last time we be with each other. I wanted to tell them how much they meant to me. I never did. The whole situation reminded me of when I delayed telling my mother what I felt until it was too late. That burden had eaten away at my independence then the streets happened and I no longer gave a damn.

Juicy by the Notorious BIG thumped loud and we all related. Maybe it was the champagne or the weed but my mind fell into reminiscing. I sat down with my head spinning, drifting like a log wood in an ocean of thoughts as them niggas moved on with the talk of broads.

"I'd be fucking da bitch and da bitch so loud, she wakes up her mother and she joined us in da bed. I was bangin' both…"

The celebration was a loud, boastful goodbye to our clique. It reminded me of when we committed to making real cheddar. The year 2000 was a grand hustle time, everyone flossed with a gun and I had two, just in case. I knew being gangster took heart and I wanted to show these niggas out here that I was someone to be reckoned with.

On the streets, one slip and cops or niggas be salivating, waiting to bag you. I put the .22 in my Timberland boots and the 9 millie in my waistband. Fuck the jackers and the cops. I'm prepared to go to war and die if niggas fuck with family, my money or my crew.

All the meetings would be on the Ave over at Squeeze's rest. That nigga had a huge fucking crib and he had the 70" Plasma joint. We had come a long way from babies wrestling in the park to straight up mobbing.

It was lovely back then, plenty sunshine and pretty ladies going by. Some on their way to work, others seemed in a rush to get to nowhere. One morning, I spotted one as I drove slowly in my silver 745 BMW. I crept and watched as she swished her hips from side to side.

She knew my eyes were following her every motion. So she brushed her long, light-brown, hair wavy on her slightly exposed shoulders. About five foot six, I was all over that. One thing was clear; she wasn't a hood rat. I saw the look in her dark Spanish eyes and I knew what she wanted. She wanted a man that was romantic.

Up ahead, I knew there was florist on Atlantic Ave. I pulled up to the curb, hopped out the Beemer and ran into the flower store. The place was crowded, the only clerks were too busy trimming and wrapping flowers at the counter. I looked around and saw the perfect bunch of white and yellow roses inside the display door. The sign read $30 per dozen. I glanced quickly over my shoulders at the busy clerks. They were still too busy to even see me grab the flowers and run back to the Beemer.

She walked so sexily that I could feel my dick starting

to rise. Bouncing hips built for sexing. With pleasure I watched her then got in the car and drove away. Tracking her through my rearview, it was clear she looked good enough for me to go all the way. Everything was in place; her hair, a little tan to go with that caramel tone made her complexion perfect and she had a gorgeous face set off by some luscious lips. This broad was a dime. And you know I drove slowly peeking at that ass because that was what first caught my attention.

Her bootie rolled around while her shapely legs vigorously strolled into my life. It was one of them exciting asses that easily bounced around with no visible effort. Love to fuck that, I thought as my plan was hatched. I was convinced that she couldn't resist this game I was about to spit.

I drove further up the block and pulled over and popped my collar. There I waited leaning against the whip, stunting with a bunch of flowers in my hand. The way my jewels shone, you could tell that this wasn't 'How to be a Player 101.' From the 22 inch-shoes on the BMW to the $10,000 piece on my neck, I was a lover indeed, truly balling with no stress.

I looked at the iced out Roly, frosty on my wrist. It was 8:30. That meant that I'd have time to get my game on and make it to Squeeze's crib. Recently, since he had to care for his seed, Promise had fallen into the habit of being late in the mornings. He had mad love for his seed and that nigga had to go through that morning routine with her. It was the type of situation that makes a nigga go soft. You know, lose heart, and start to think of getting out of the game cuz of responsibilities. That kinda shit gotta make a hard nigga mush but it doesn't really matter, he was Promise. So I knew I definitely wouldn't be the last to arrive.

Squeeze, he'll always be there on time, loud as ever be

and ready for whatever. Him and his crack-head-for-a uncle, they be getting on the nerves with all that arguing in the morning. I know for sure that that nigga Show would always be late any fucking how.

Show had bad bed tendencies. He be wanting to lay around watching Jerry Springer with his baby momma all day long. That nigga was the white man's best friend. His lazy ass will still be sleeping when the revolution goes down. Nigga lived a block away from Squeeze and was never on time.

Me, I wanted this gorgeous ass broad coming my way and I licked my lips cause I knew I had the time to pitch my game. I saw that smile slowly sneak out as she approached. Her body language said she was impressed.

"Hey good morning, mami. How are you doing?" I greeted as she approached.

She said nothing at first but I saw her glance at the BMW and the shoes it sat on. She smiled when she saw the bling on my wrist and pinkie. Chicken-head, I thought as I offered her the flowers.

"Nice car," she said in an unimpressed tone, not even taking the flowers.

"What's your name, beautiful?"

"Natasha and yours?"

"They call me Pooh, baby. Need a lift to work?"

"No, I'm good, thank you Pooh," she said and I couldn't tell if she was joking or not. The broad was playing me.

"What about the flowers?" I asked and the broad gave me a blasé look.

"What're those for?" she asked with that stank attitude. She reached for flowers and took them. I peeked down her dress to look at her breasts. I handed her the flowers and noticed her shine. I checked the rest of her gear. She had a Fendi bag and smelled really nice, so I ignored all of the warning signs and kicked it.

"Flowers for a beautiful senorita, ma. Your perfume is very enchanting. What is it called?" I asked with a smile that couldn't be ignored.

"Ma-man, will you mind your damn bizness," she arrogantly replied.

I couldn't believe what I was hearing. Maybe my game was just flat this morning?

"Huh uh?" was the only response I could mutter.

This broad had mad fucking attitude, I thought. She was carrying a bag with Burger King and coffee. A working girl, she had a little job and big attitude.

"Ma," I started with my plea staring into her eyes. "I want you to know that I've been dreaming about sump'n fine as you coming in my life. And tell me this is true so I can go and get the biggest ice from Jake's."

"Save all that ying yang, my man. Can't you see that you've got to come with sump' a little better than that."

I was undaunted by this fine looking broad. The question that popped in my confused mind: Was she worth the challenge? They all come running eventually, these women you meet on the streets. They all had a breaking point. I kept searching, wanting to find hers.

"You're right. I know a girl as beautiful as you probably get these proposals all day long. So give me your number, and I'll give you a call and you and me can discuss this later over some dinner at the Four Seasons. Maybe we could catch a late flick and spend the night in the Penthouse suite at the Trump International. I could do all that, ma."

"I'm not some hoochie who's gonna fall for all that bullshit," she said and looked at her watch. It was filled with stones and so too was the bracelet on her wrist. I had no choice but to use my gun.

"Ma, I want you to take off all your jewelry and give them to me."

"Huh?" she asked looking stunned.

It was her time to be speechless. I brought the weapon closer to her ample chest. I think I saw her nipples rise and stick out like headlights. It was obvious this broad had seen a gun up close and personal before she didn't even blink.

"Bitch, now you playing deaf?" I asked. "Take off all ya fucking jewelry and pass them to me. Right now, bitch!" I yelled, scaring her. She started doing as I ordered but real slow like this was a game of striptease.

There at the street corner, on a beautiful day, I relieved this stuck-up-ass-bitch with-attitude of all her jewels and took her Fendi bag. I emptied the bag onto the passenger side of the car and returned the empty bag to her. She had that shock look of disbelief all over her face.

"Need a ride to work bitch?" I asked as if we were friends going on our separate ways for the day. She shook her head and stood rooted to the spot.

"Ahight then, just go ahead and have a lovely day," I said jumping into the car.

Tires screeched and I was out. I left her standing there still frozen in a state of shock.

"Bi-i-yotch!" I yelled and tore up the road on my way to

Squeeze's block. I pulled up and jumped out with breakfast and flowers. Just outside the building was a bus stop. An elderly lady stood patiently waiting for the next bus. I offered the bunch of flowers to her.

She took them smiled and said, "God bless you, young man. How did you know it was my birthday?"

"A birdie just told me," I smiled and walked to the building.

I rang the bell three times. Squeeze's crack head Uncle Junior let me into the apartment. I gave him some daps and continued to look at all the credit cards lifted earlier from the most beautiful girl in the world.

"What da fuck's a damn W4?" I asked Squeeze.

"Yo whassup wid your man, Promise, son? I swear that nigga gon be late for his own muthafucking funeral, son," Squeeze said, ignoring my question.

"That nigga be having executive hours, son. Talking 'bout his daughter had to go to muthafucking preschool," Show said walking from the bathroom. "Let me get one o' 'em sausage biscuits, Pooh." I was surprised that Show was there, actually early for a change.

"Easy man, I'm fucking starving nigga. That broad kept me up all fucking night. Had to put that broad to bed. Wake up and my dick is still in her mouth, ready," I said. "I need my energy, dogs."

"Yeah, what you need is to do is give a nigga a sausage biscuit and I'll hook you up wid some mu'fucking tiger bone."

"Man, what da fuck is a tiger bone?"

"Let me tell you son, you really don't wanna fuck with that shit. I fucked ugly ass Sarah on the beach at Coney Island off that shit, son."

There was a major pause in the room. All three of us looked at each other blankly.

"You fucked ugly ass Sarah?" I asked finally.

"Yeah, son, that Tiger Bone…."

"Don't be blaming that shit on no Tiger bone, dogs. That's straight…"

"Ah, see, you don't know nothing bout that. That's some shit for you," Show, said laughing.

"You don't wanna fuck with that, young un. Your young ass done kill a bitch with that shit inside o' you," Squeeze said laying out some weed. "This some good shit right here, son."

"That Tiger Bone ain't gonna have me skeetin' off on no ugly broads and that's fer sure."

"Whatever…this hydro is what's up."

"Word, it's that raw or what?"

"I got some at the crib, son," Show said. "Give me a sausage biscuit and I'll break yer young ass some."

"Fuck that nigga! If that shit is like Viagra or sump'n then I don't need that kinda help, dog. Just give me a good-looking broad wid a nice ass and I could handle myself. Twist that Dutch, Squeeze."

"Yeah, speaking of a nice bitch, I saw yer physical this morning on her way to school," Show said. "I swear that her ass looks kinda fat. It's ready, son."

No sooner than the words had escaped Show's lips, I was all over him, the 9mm in my hand.

"Ahight, you got jokes, right? Let's hear how we laugh when this gun's in your mouth, nigga. Fat muthafucka!" I said, grabbing my crotch.

"Y'all be easy!" Squeeze yelled. "Show, here's the key to the ride. Here, catch this dog. Go to Mickey D's or wherever, bring me back some breakfast too, nigga. Go and stop fucking around like you gonna kill each other over breakfast from Burger King," Squeeze said and took out another sack of weed.

"Is that what I think it is?" I asked looking at the purple stuff.

Squeeze smiled and poured some out before yelling. "Yeah nigga, this from that white boy out there in New Jeroose." Squeeze said then he began gently fondling the weed the way you would do to some new ass, Squeeze started running his mouth. "Oh yeah baby, this the bomb shit. This that Canada Dro shit," Squeeze said looking up, "And I know where we can get some more o' this. Oh baby, it's so easy."

"Word?" I asked taking the plastic bag and inhaling the scent of the green smoky material. "It's sticky fer sure," I managed to say, my mouth salivating for more.

"That it is, bay-Pooh. That it is," Squeeze said.

By the time Show and Promise came through, Squeeze and me had smoked about two blunts a piece. I was getting open off the dro when the three rings of doorbell broke the spell.

"Doorbell," I said yelling above the loud surround sound from his home theater system.

"It's probably them niggas. Get the door, Pooh."

I put the blunt down and walked to the door. Just before the entrance and off to the left was the kitchen with a security cam monitor. I peeked just in case then I buzzed the door.

"Yeah it was them," I said checking the name on the credit card stolen from the cutie.

"Promise wid him?" Squeeze asked.

"Yeah, da nigga's coming-up too," I replied.

Once again, becoming engrossed sifting through all the credit cards. Her name was on a W4 form. I asked, "What the hell is a W4?" I showed the form to Squeeze. He was older; he should know what it was. I waited too long for the answer. "Man gimme that…"

"Chill, I'm trying to see what the shit sez," he answered.

"If you don't know just say you don't know, nigga. You ain't got to be embarrassed round me. We boys, dogs," I said.

"Yeah nigga, this got sump'n to do with slavery and I ain't going back to that," he said not fully comprehending the information on the form. Squeeze didn't want to admit it.

"I hear you, dogs. Maybe Promise will know. You can't know everything," I said.

Squeeze threw the paper back at me before continuing. "It got sump'n to do wid some kinda tax bullshit or sump'n like that," he said sounding frustrated. He put pressure on himself like that because Squeeze actually believed that despite not finishing any type of formal school training, he knew everything. No one could tell him nothing. He had a lot to learn, we all did. I didn't take it that personal.

"Whassup, whassup," the glad hands started when Promise and Show walked through the door. Like real family members, we'd embrace first every time we saw each other. It was always that way.

We had been shorties on the block, developed our own handshake and embraced each other right to left. It was unlike what anyone else was doing. It made us belong, call it gang-related or whatever, going through the ritualistic embraces meant all was forgiven. And besides making us feel like we belonged to something, no one else had it, it really made us unique.

Through the years, no matter how large the booty got, we kept things civil between the members. That was a lot due to how Show was. Big, black, and ugly, Show was the enforcer. He was down to getting in a nigga's face at the drop of a dime.

They all walked into the apartment. Show was in the midst of stuffing a Mickey D's breakfast sandwich into his huge mouth, when he and then Promise walked in. They both carried food bags.

"Yo, does any o' y'all niggas know what da fuck is a W4?" I asked and waited but all I got was chomping sounds accompanied by slurps of three hungry niggas feasting. "Ain't nobody trying to help me out?"

"That some shit that America is using to destroy Saddam," Show said. "We need that shit, son."

"Whatever nigga," I responded. Everyone else chuckled.

"What y'all niggas watching?" Show asked, changing the subject.

"Nigga, can't you see the news is on the mu'fucking telly, mu'fucka?" Squeeze said then added, "Nigga, you best go get your eyes checked because you're blind. The TV is only 'bout seventy wide."

"Word, Show, you need to get you bifocals. I wouldn't want your blind ass putting a cap in the wrong ass."

"Nigga, please, all I'm saying is change the channel, nigga. You know the news ain't nothing but some bullshit anyway."

"Ahight, here is da remote. You find sump'n else," Squeeze said handing something that looked like a small computer to Show.

He pressed a couple of the knobs, familiar with it as if we

were at the arcade and he was hogging the video game. Finally the reverberation of G-Unit sounds *How To Rob A MC* penetrated the room, framing each corner with the picture of the happy gangster family. My question was now buried beneath the need to eat. We were like brothers, able to laugh at each other's faults while we enjoyed the spoils.

I remember attending school and hearing other classmates boast about their fathers, the cop, the janitor, the lawyer, the dentist. I even knew a few who had dads that were locked up in jail. I had no memory of having a father.

At the age of four years, one evening after coming home from school, I decided to ask my mother about my dad then changed my mind. I was afraid what the answer was gonna be. Maybe it was better not to know. It wasn't until six years later when I couldn't take it anymore that I finally gathered enough courage to venture there with my mother.

"Mommy, do I have a father?" I asked not realizing at the time that I was opening a whole can of worms.

"Don't be so stupid, Paul. Everyone has to have a mother and a father. That is how life is created, boy. No wonder your damn friends call you Pooh-Pooh," she answered with a smile.

"I know that and my friends don't call me Pooh-Pooh. It's just Pooh," I said furiously. "Why can't you just tell me that I don't have a dad instead of trying to be so smart," I said angrily, stomping my feet and demanding the truth.

I may have learned something but it wasn't what I wanted. I found out that yelling at my mother and getting her angry will cause her to throw that nice flower vase at my head. Especially after she had her drink and smokes. Whatever! I was out the room and never mentioned it again. It stayed on my mind and

I calculated how I would get her to tell me but gave up instead. Maybe it was lack of courage or maybe I just gave up caring.

Through the years, I saw my mother as a woman who just couldn't keep men and maybe that was why my father never stayed. My mother had different men and each would last about two or three months in the relationship. She would start saying things then and you know a nigga be quick to leave.

Mother was a nagging woman who quickly grew on you. I can't say there was any real family unity but I had nothing but love for the family God had blessed me with. If there were any questions, they were my family in name but out here on the street, my real family was the niggas in this room and my two guns for protection.

My sister, Lindsay and me had different fathers. Her father, Kenneth Roberts, lived with us for a minute. He was cool at first, buying me Jordan sneaks and fresh gear. Every Saturday, he would take us to the Fulton Mall and we'd really be cool. I was about ten years old and he was such a good man, I almost start calling him daddy.

Three months later he moved in with us and my mother started nagging and everything just changed. During the six months he lived with us, our mall trips went from every Saturday to once a while till he moved out. After that we never saw him again. When we'd asked about him like, "Hey mom, what's up with you and Kenny?" she'd look at us with seething eyes and roll them at us.

"Kenny's dead," she said.

You can't blame anyone for the way you live your life, my mother always said, "You got to get da fuck up out of here if you're not going to school or paying rent."

I had my clique. From day one, we were down for each other. I watched their greedy mugs put the finishing touch to breakfast.

"Yo, lets get into some big-dog biz. Uncle, get da fuck out. This is not for your ears."

His uncle would disappear and we'd be four smoking kids grown into men. We ran the streets when everyone was coming up and we respected each other so much that we were like a real family. Promise and Squeeze were like older brothers and Big Show was all muscles, no brain. They all tried to protect me. I was like their baby brother and none of the bullies touched me.

These ghetto soldiers were my peeps and although I didn't want to see them leave, I wanted what was best for them. I knew Promise, he'd be a good dad, and Show and Promise would probably raise their babies. I could see them pushing strollers and wondering what type of toys to get.

I yearned for my dad but knew that I'd probably never see the bastard. Stepfathers were the closest I'd come to having any type of role models. The nigs from the hood were my real family. It was hard to feel like you could never hustle with them anymore. Everything must come to an end, and anything that's really, really sweet, hurts even more when it's time to let it go.

I remember when my stepfather would go off to work everyday. My mom and little sister would hope that he would make it back home. I would hope he didn't. It was that shameless contradiction I wore like bling. I hated any man who tried to be my father even though I may have wanted them to stick around for my mother.

"Go to school," he would tell me when he'd try to play dad.

I used to believe in him until my mom told me he did all he'd accomplished with no high school education. When I found out that he didn't even have a high school diploma, he couldn't tell me nada. He'd try and offer the excuse that in his time, blacks weren't allowed to go to school. I'd leave the apartment early pretending that I was going to school but then I wouldn't go.

The reason was the distraction of the streets and the paper that had to be chased. Being poor, you had a choice to either stay that way or fool yourself into thinking that working for someone else was gonna make you rich. We were down for that dollar bill and we specialized in taking everything yours.

If a nigga cut any deal in the hood, we'd be part of it. Whether it be selling drugs or guns, we wanted in. The pimps were targets too. Taking their money off their ho's, lifting that dough out their snatch that was my specialty. Yeah, we did everything to make the streets ours.

Even though I breathe gangster, it hadn't always been that way. I remember being a shorty and madukes worrying all the time that her men would never stay in her life. They'd be around for awhile but after couple months she would start whining and wake up from having dreams about them leaving. Then just like that, they wouldn't be back.

I didn't tell her that the reason they never came back was because she was always bitching at them. I just tried to explain to her that men don't like when they home and their women constantly be jawing. Any real man will leave and make home somewhere else. Maybe I said it all wrong. She wasn't trying to hear me. I finally told her after I'd hear enough of her.

"Ma, you just bitch too much, man," I said as I sat at the dinner table. We had just finished eating dinner; fried chicken, corn, and rice. The television was tuned to my mother's favorite show, *Sanford and Son* reruns. My younger sister, Lindsay, was helping with the dishes. I didn't see the need for me to help. Madukes never saw it my way and jumped under my skin.

"What, you don't think you should be participating in the damn house chores?" She asked me.

But I was busy playing my Game Boy. Instinctively, I ignored her. That's when shit hit the fan and she started really yelling.

"You lazy cocksucker, you never do anything around here but sleep. What you think? You got a staff of maids or sump'n?"

I tried to ignore her telling myself it was just madukes. I tried holding my head but she got louder and aggravated the fuck out of me.

"You're always fucking screaming. Why?" I asked.

She was surprised by my reaction but kept going anyhow. I had to put a stop to it once and for all. I always respected my mother, let that be understood, but when she started berating me in front of my younger sister, that was total disrespect and peace didn't exist no more.

"You're such a lazy bastard. You don't work and can't even hold down a damn job. You're good for nothing," she yelled.

"You fucking bitch," I said, seething. "You wanna know the fuck why you can't get a fucking man to stay with you?" I asked with the bravery of a fool. Her face registered fear and I pointed my finger menacingly at her as I continued, "That's because you're a fucking bitch, that's why." I realized then that I couldn't take it back.

That was the beginning of the end for me living in that apartment with my family. It happened during a major fight when everyone goes all out and to the winner the spoils. But there were no winners here. The street was our benefactor. Now, I knew I had to go and really hustle for a living.

My sister, Lindsay, stared wide-eyed at me. Maybe she was embarrassed by all of this but we both were becoming older. Lindsay was in the 10th grade and was aware of mommy's temper. Her irritability along with an innate bitchy attitude was all it took for explosions after explosions. Neither of us had the guts to tell her until now.

"Come on, stop this yelling and cursing the two of you," Lindsay said but neither of us heeded her request. That night, I left and slept at Squeeze's. My nigga looked out for the night.

"Yo, so why the fuck you and your old earth be going at it, son?" he asked as he passed the blunt.

"Squeeze, dead up, I be chilling, doing nothing, you feel me? That bitch she just old and tired, man."

I smoke and passed the night away. The next morning I saw my sister downstairs on her way to school. She told me about what had happened after I'd left home the day before.

"Pooh, Show called and mommy wants to know where'd you spend the night? She was worried over you. You ain't call or nothing," Lindsay said. "Gimme a few bucks," she added before she walked away. I pulled out a wad of bills and gave her couple twenty-dollar bills. "Thanks." She kissed me and was off to school.

That was a good thing, it turned out that she liked school. I didn't. I walked slowly up the stairs and went into my ma-dukes apartment and sat on the bed, still feeling the weed from last night. It wasn't too long after before sparks started to fly.

"You smell like weed, your eyes are brown, you're high,"

she said bringing the noise to the quiet high of my room. I just gave her that stare which read I don't care.

"You're a fucking loser," she continued. "Don't you see all your friends going to school? But you wanna play Mr. Bad Man and not go. Well, I'm not gonna be around for ever and..."

I never gave her the chance to finish. I'd heard enough. "Shut da fuck up, bitch!" I yelled.

"You need to get fuck up out of ma place, Pooh," she said spitting venom. "Get the fuck up 'fore I call the police and tell them you dealin' drugs. Don't think I don't know."

I don't know if I was just scared about my mother calling the cops or what. I left for good shortly after she threw me out. About a week later, my sister contacted me telling me mommy missed me and how much she was worried about me. She wanted to know when I was gonna be coming back.

"Over my dead body, never. I ain't never going back," I said.

"She wanted you to know your room is there and you're always welcome." We'd sit in Burger King and talk and I always made sure to break them off from my hustle.

I loved madukes but she really got on my last nerves with her man problems and her useless griping. I was 17 years old, living on my own, and things weren't bad so I gave my sister five hundred dollars and kissed her goodbye. I figured as long as she had my number, we'd be cool. But I wanted away from madukes. That bitch was crazy, fuckin' locá.

I never did too much drugs. I was strictly a baller destined to be the next Jordan but I never fully recovered from a severe knee injury and that put a strain on the basketball career. Since I couldn't ball, school became a drag so I quit.

I first got started at fifteen grinding in front of the buildings. They made me a lookout. My job all day was to just hang out and to steer clientele my man's way and let them know when jakes were near. Two fingers raised high and my peeps would get rid of their works and be out. We developed early warning systems that would go off if police came around and we stayed off those street phones.

Whether they were plainclothes or uniforms, the police had that distinct look and smell. I could sniff them a mile away. No one got bagged on my shift. I did that for two months and that was the period of my apprenticeship on the streets of New York.

By the time I was eighteen, I had established a small ring; getting coke and selling it to the Dominicans. Then hit them up for weed and sell it to the Jamaicans two times above the cost. I'd hustled everything you gave me. Broads I messed with knew what was up. I'd be quick to send one of them to distract a customer just in case the product wasn't too good. A nigga be too busy looking down the bitches dress to even notice a switch.

I'd have them roll blunts with a particular degree of hydro then slip him a pound or two of something else. Suckers never found out until it was too late then I would always promise to make it up. They wouldn't remember because I would send two more badass broads to deliver. You get the picture. The streets had made it that easy.

There were some rough times like when we hit them cats from Tompkins Houses and the following day, them niggas bagged me on my way from a diner. That was crazy. I'd just dropped a broad to the train station. I was sitting in the ride rolling sump'n and listening to music. I got hungry so I decided to walk down to a diner on the corner.

The niggas was coming from the diner and one of them recognized me. They approached me like they were po-po.

"Yo, ain't you one a them mothafucka from yesterday who jacked us, dog?"

"I don't know what da fuck y'all got going on but you better back down nigga. I ain't the one," I said and before I could reach for the iron, someone cold clocked me.

I staggered to the middle of the street and felt couple more blows to my head. Backing up, I slowly paced myself not wanting to trip but not being able to turn and run because them niggas would shoot me in the back. I felt blood dripping down my cheek. I gripped the nine milli.

"Ahight, y'all niggas want it?" I asked waving my weapon. I had to show 'em that I wasn't no punk. Niggas dove to the side as I let off couple rounds. "Ahight, y'all don't want none o' this," I said and ran when I saw five-oh coming toward us.

I quickly located my car, jumped in and hit reverse. The BM flew down a one-way, barely avoiding three parked cars on the right side of the road. My gear was soaked with blood. I checked the mirror. It wasn't as bad as it looked, but I had a bloody lip and my face was fucked up.

There were no cops following as I eased onto Atlantic and headed to Squeeze. I got on the horn and hollered to holler at Squeeze. No one picked up on that side. Where were them niggas when you need them, I wondered. I had to find them and warn my ghetto soldiers.

By the time I arrived at Squeeze's place, my face had swollen up more and looked worse than it felt. I checked down in the basement after ringing his bell upstairs. Niggas were in the basement. Someone buzzed me inside and when I barged in; the whole shit broke loose. Everyone was kinda fucked up behind that.

"Wha' da fuck! Niggas bum-rushed us. Get your combat gears we going to war. We got to go see bout 'em boys." Squeeze was ready to ride and that's the type of soldier you could count on. As I went to the bathroom and cleaned my face, I could see a worried frown on Promise's mug. He was getting softer for real.

We rode on them niggas and again the cops saved their asses. But not before shots lit up their blocks making the whole place hot like the fourth of July. In a few minutes, an army of swat was at our backs. We had to get the fuck up out with the quickness.

Later, the nigga, frontin' ass Promise, wanted to be let out by his ride. Squeeze pulled up along the X5. The nigga quickly jumped out like he was shook and bounced. I'm thinking we going back to the rest to strategize on these niggas but I guess that wasn't the plan. That wasn't what Promise had in mind.

"I'll holla at you later, my nigga."

"Ahight dogs," Promise said without so much as even giving anyone dap. No love, he was out with the quickness. I rode the shotgun slumped in silence.

"Yo, the nigga Promise turning into mush," I said and meant every word.

No one responded but I knew it had to be on everyone's mind here sitting in the truck. It was plain as day. Promise was walking away from us. I wasn't gonna be kissing that nigga's ass trying to be a sucker and all. If it was over, it was over. That's all there was to that.

"Squeeze pull over here, let me grab a brew, nig," I said.

Squeeze steered to the curb by the corner store and I

hopped out.

"Anybody want anything from the store?" I asked.

"Bring back a six pack," Show shouted. Squeeze just nodded is head.

I walked into the store feeling like Promise had in some way let me down. The old heads had told me to respect the set. Promise had disrespected-big time. I copped the beer and left the store.

The three of us sat in the SUV outside Squeeze rest steaming blunt after blunt and listening to Talib Kwele, *Just to Get By.* No one was really in a talkative mood. I guess there wasn't anything much left to be said. We were like lovers torn. The streets had blessed us as a set. But now we were slowly drifting apart. I drank my beer feeling pathetic with a bitter taste in my mouth. I didn't wanna welcome the stay of the feeling so I made a move.

"Y'all brothers be safe," I said after guzzling my last beer.

"What, you out? Ya gonna be ahight, young un?" I gave Show a hug and gave Squeeze a pound.

"You're leavin' for real nig? Yo why don't you chill and watch the game or sump'n?" Squeeze asked.

"Nah, I'm out dogs. I'm a go fuck wid a broad. Be easy y'all," I said with my thoughts in a flurry and jumped out the SUV.

"Yeah lil' nig, we gon see you in a minute, ahight."

"Ahight," I said as I reached my car and turn on the ignition. The realization hit me hard. I didn't want the feel of coldness that comes with being alone so I put in a call to an old flame in Queens. I was in need of some TLC. She answered eager just like I thought.

"I'm sayin' who dis callin me and I took a look at my caller-ID and I just knew it was your fine ass. What's popping, sugar?"

She asked with tail-wagging curiosity.

"What's good, Charisma? I need you baby."

"You do baby, Pooh?"

"Yeah, I had an ill accident, and gotta lay low for a minute, you know how a brotha do?"

"And you know your girl, Charisma's here for you my sweetheart. Come on through. I ain't got nothin' but time, baby. I'll make you some o' momma soup and if that doesn't work, you know momma will give you sump'n else that'll soothe ya."

"Say no more, ma," I said and headed to the BQE for Queens.

She was my bottom broad, the type who respected my intuition. Never too nosy, Charisma played her position. She respected my grind and trusted my instincts. I got there soon and saw her captivating smile, her smooth, dark skin. Charisma was built with plenty junk in the trunk. When she moved, sexuality was oozing from her tight poom-poom shorts.

She greeted me with a wet kiss when I walked inside the one bedroom apartment. After washing me well, Charisma licked me up and down as soon as my wife-beater was off. Slobbin' my dick down, I exploded skeetin' all over face. Skism filled with my children drippin' hot and thick all over the side of Charisma's delighted face. Later, she wiped me down.

The next seven days, I chilled with Charisma. True to her word, she revitalized me with that good stew her momma taught her to make. Stretching my jimmy and stamina to the limit, Charisma worked me out well. Everyday the wisdom gave me brains as soon as his majesty divine was up. Her tongue took me out of this world like I never been before. And, oh yeah, the stew was off the meat rack.

Couple weeks later, early on a Saturday morning, I was alone with Charisma jotting down prose, when the phone started ringing off the hook. No one besides fam had this number so it had to be one of my peeps. My palms sweated and there was a surge of electricity traveling from my bowels. I paused hesitating before picking up the phone.

"Who dis...?"

Hearing the familiar voice of Squeeze gave me the chills as he brought the lowdown on Promise and some new broad he was fucking with. Squeeze swagger was on high when the conversation changed to buying a nightclub in BK. He chatted excitedly.

"Yeah, babe bro we gonna own sump'n legit stack some paper and keep poppin' bottles..."

We planned to meet up in da club early and look things over. I decided to check the joint out later. I put down the cellphone and continued to write.

Charisma didn't want me to leave her place just yet, but I had to go. She was all over kissing me like it was the last time.

"You don't have to go," Charisma said.

"I'll be back," I said in between sucks on her lips.

"Do me a favor and just take care of yourself, Pooh," she said.

"I will, ma," I said leaving out the door.

Later, I went out on the courts but left the hustling early. I rode out to East Flatbush to Nelson's Barbershop and met Tech outside.

"What's poppin' Tech?"

"Baby Pooh, how're you? I ain't seen you in a minute," Tech greeted.

"Been chillin," I answered. "What you got new?"

"I got some Biggie remix, it's fire, kid."

"I better cop that then," I said taking the CD and walking into the barbershop.

The place was buzzing with customers but I hit Nelson with a twenty spot and he jumped me in the line. As soon as I sat down in the chair he started with his preaching.

"What up Nel?"

"Pooh, what's good I ain't seen you in a while," Nelson said.

"I been chillin', laying low, man..."

"Now Pooh, I known you a long muthafuckin' time and I heard you been up to no good," Nelson started in a low whisper.

"Nel man, you can't believe everything you hear, man," I countered.

"I know but think about what you getting into. You got a mother and sister. You can't be living dangerously, you have to be the man in the house."

"I'm good man. I be taking care of madukes and all..."

"I ain't saying you're not, I'm just saying be cool. You've got to live right. Start paying attention to school and all that, you feel me...?"

"School ain't for everyone, Nel. My sister is still going though, man. She ahight."

"That's good to know but you gotta make a change. Stop hanging with them gangstas on the Ave..."

"I'm chill, Nel. I'll be ahight, man."

"Chill my ass. I hear shit happening on the street. You ridin' in 'em fast cars with 'em fast girls and all that fast money. I'm a tell you like my mother used to tell me, live fast die young, you feel me, young 'un?"

"Yeah, yeah, ahight," I chuckled.

I glanced up at the mirror. Nelson hook a brother up but he be going on too much with his lecturing. I was glad his preaching would soon be over. Nelson put the final touches on my dome and I was fresh for later.

"Spray some o' that sweet smelling shit on it," I said and hit him with another twenty.

"Good looking out, but you already hit me, Pooh."

"I know man, that's for all the lessons you droppin…" I smiled and was on my way out the door.

"Yo Nel man, you can't tell these young 'uns what to do. They ain't listening to you." I heard Rick saying as the door to the barbershop closed.

"Word up…" a customer said.

"But does that mean we should stop tryin'," Nelson shot back. "Back in the days someone older than me was trying to keep me out of jailhouse and the morgue, you feel me?"

"I hear you but it's 2002 and it's different times now," Rick said.

I didn't want to hear anymore B.S. and copped couple more CD's from Tech. Just as I was about to hop into my Beemer, I heard Sincere.

"Yo, young G, what's up?"

"Sincere, how're you, son?"

"I seen you in some hours, young G. What's been goin' on?"

I didn't wanna say too much as I saw Tech's ears perked up, and stood next my ride and waited for Tyrone. He was one of the privileged kids who used to mock me before I dropped school. Now we were both hustling on the streets of BK, and my clique, my game, my money was mad tighter than anything he could dream.

"Yo that BM is smashing..."

"It's the new seven four five, son. Copped it last month."

I watched as Tyrone's hand ecstatically caressed my whip like it was some fine-ass broad.

"Wha...this shit like what..."

"Traded in the three and paid sixty-five cash money for this bitch," I announced with my swagger was way high. "It's fully loaded all automatic, son and I got them twenty-fours for like another twenty."

"Damn! You da fuckin man," Tyrone gushed.

"How you rollin'?"

"Trying get like you," he answered. I took it as an apology.

"Yo this my boy, CJ," he said pounding my arm out of socket.

"What up? I'm Pooh," I said extending my arm and blinding them both with ice.

"CJ, what's good?" His boy replied, sheepishly trying very hard not to seem too overwhelmed.

I knew I was in another league. The frost I was carrying chill when Tyrone started jocking like a gold digging bitch.

"Yo man , Pooh you gotta put me down. Give me your math please so I can get down, man."

"No need for a all that, Ty. You know where I be, come see me like Monday or sump'n. I got work for you."

"Ahight, ok sir. That's what da fuck I'm talkin' bout hook a nigga up."

His boy, CJ held a frown like he was hatin'.

"Yo man, CJ, you can come work for me too. I got enough works, son," I smiled.

CJ nodded and looked inside the whip as I opened the door. They were saying sump'n to each other I decided it was time to slide off. Like Biz Markie said, *"Damn it feels good to see peoples all up on it..."*

I gave them both daps and hopped in the BMW, peeling out. They stood gawking, Tyrone's mouth wide opened, while CJ wore the frown of a hater. Fuck what they thought! I knew *they caught the vapors*. My wheels were spinning as I tore down Flatbush Avenue. I stopped and copped another bracelet before sliding back to the crib to get ready for later.

I was dope by myself but ten times more when I hung with my crew. It had been awhile since we were all together. There was a kind of good feeling surrounding the phone call. It was a chance for all of us to get back together. For the past couple weeks, everybody had fallen back and laid low.

Promise and Squeeze had us chillin' for a minute. All along I wasn't rockin' with that flow. I was hooked to the daily grindin' on the streets of BK. Now that summer was here and things were beginning to warm up, niggas wanted to be out and about making moves again. At least that's what I thought.

The time would be right again for us to see each other. I'd go down see them later and have a few drinks. It was Friday night and everything was off and jumpin' in NYC. There was no other place I'd want to see. Because of the hot summer air everyone was out on the streets tonight. The phone rang and this time it was my sister.

"Hi, Pooh what's poppin'?"

"What's good, Lindsay? How's my lil' sis?"

"Fine, I'm doing fine. Mom says to tell you hello."

"Tell ma I sez hi." My response made me think I kinda missed the old earth. "What y'all up to, love?" I asked quickly changing the conversation from madukes.

I'd never received a message before from my mother through Lindsay. I knew my sister be faking sometimes but I went along with it. I listened to her as I walked around coordinating my gear.

"Just chilling, chilling. It's dumb hot over on this side. How's it over there?" My sister asked.

She was in a small talk way trying to say something but not saying it. She probably wanted some money and couldn't ask because my mother was staring at her. I'd stop by if I could.

"The same way it is over there steamy hot. Sis I gotta take a shower. I'll try and stop by. See ya later," I said trying to rush off the phone but she wouldn't let me.

"Pooh, Pooh, mommy said to tell you to be careful, alright? I'll speak to you again. Bye," Lindsay said and I could hear the dial tone as I stood looking at the telephone.

Not stopping to think too much of it, I headed to the shower. I knew that them niggas would be fly so I went into my closet and got fresh from head to toe in black. Versace shirt, Evisu jeans and Gucci kicks. Dressed to the nines, I left the crib at a little past eleven.

I was frosty with a blunt of hash mixed with that bomb-bomb-zee in my hand and the nine in my waist. I drove slowly in the shiny, silver BM. Looking like a million bucks, I kept my eyes peeled for jakes and jackas watching me. Nothing was poppin' off on da block, just the same ol' hustlers, runners and heads from the drug game. I watched them through my rear-view.

Boops blew by as I drove slowly down the Ave., lights flashing aiming to stop the next man. I u-turned easy knowing I was dirty, holding heat and a blunt in my hand. No matter how much hush money I'd offer that cop that mu'fucka ain't taking it and I ain't going to nobody's jailhouse tonight.

I wouldn't miss that DT's head if that nigga came at me. I'd practiced shooting that head off in my dreams ever since I was a baby boy. I'd see team of cops like gangs roaming the hood. They'd ride through the hood like they ain't want you to forget who really running shit.

It's funny how whenever I got dressed up I'd do a drive through the hood listening to Jay Z spit lyrically on a track with the great Biggie Smalls.

Jigga. Bigga Nigga how you figga/ Hey yo peep the style and they way the cop sweat us.../

Jay Z ripped the track as my thoughts tried to keep up. I could see all the small changes in the hood and wondered why I didn't just get out. Dressed as I was I could get into a college or sump'n. I probably could find a nice respectable wifey. I mean maybe I could really do something with my life besides my present hustle, not be just another street gangster.

Hit you back split you /Fuck fist fight and lame scuffles...

I'd floss, just a lil' sump'n while thinking of what else could I get into. I could try running my own biz, maybe set-up some crack houses and make some real cheddar. Then flip that on some legit shit and make that money work instead of tricking it all on dumb broads and mad ho's. That would be a good look, I thought as the track play-on.

*Most hated... Ill fated while y'all pump Willie I run
up in stunts silly ...scared so you sent your lil' man
to come kill me...*

Lost in my thoughts, I rode till I was in front of mom's
Brownsville housing. This wasn't planned. It had been sometime
since I had been back here. My head felt like it was on a swivel,
my eyes peeling for jackas. Finally I reached a familiar spot and
sat outside sucking on a blunt gone dead. Another ten minutes
passed before I developed the courage to go inside my mother's
apartment. I took a deep breath, ran upstairs, and rapped on her
door. Lindsay answered the door with a bright smile.

"Oh Pooh, mommy, it's Pooh. You're looking really fresh,
Pooh. You go boy..." She screamed and hugged me hard.

"Who is it?" I heard my mother yelled.

"Mommy, its Pooh. It's Pooh, I said." Lindsay shouted as
if madukes was deaf. I saw her coming from the bedroom. Then
we all met in the living room. The place looked the same but it
somehow felt smaller.

"Why did you come over tonight?" Madukes asked. I
scratched my head trying to think of the reason but none came,
so I didn't answer. "You must've known it was my birthday. I
told Lindsay not to say anything. She must've opened her big
mouth."

I could hear that distinct slur proving she'd been drinking. It
was further confirmed when I reached over to hug and kiss her.

"I ain't told you anything, right Pooh?" Lindsay screamed
from the bathroom. She came back to the living room and we all
sat around. "You looking real fine big brother."

"I knew it was sump'n why I came by. I left my sketch pad
and..."

"And your notebooks, right? Ma found them the other day and put 'em up for you."

"That's good. I'll get 'em before I go."

"You still writin' em rhymes and ah…"

"Mommy, you know that Pooh told you it was poetry, alright."

"Whateva…"

I could tell from all the chatter around me that my sister and mother missed me very much. Unfortunately I couldn't stay too long.

"Happy birthday, ma," I said and peeled off ten crisp hundred dollar bills.

She beamed when I put them in her hand and kissed her cheek. For all she'd been through, my mother didn't look old at all. The way she was dancing around the living room had me forgetting she had just turned forty.

"Pump that volume up," she yelled happy as the sound of Ludacris came on the radio. *"When I move you move…"* my mother sang along with radio. It was time for me to go. I kissed her again and my sister walked me to the door. "See ya later, Pooh," my mother yelled.

"She's riding real high because you passed-through, Pooh."

"Why you ain't reminded me it was mom's birthday?"

"Well, technically it's in a few minutes."

"Oh you mean it's tomorrow?"

"Yep, I was gonna call you again and tell you to bring her flowers and a gift. But since you're here, there's no need to."

"Nah, that's cool, Lindsay. Tomorrow I'll bring her some flowers and we'll do sump'n," I said.

"That'll be really good plus you showed up tonight. I mean nobody was expecting you to, Pooh," Lindsay said.

I kissed her soft cheek and shoved a few hundred-dollar bills in her hand. I didn't want to make this an emotional trip. I made quick on the goodbyes, hit the stairs and was out.

The night was still warm so I dropped the top to the BM and hit the Beltway on my way to the spot downtown. As soon as I pulled up, I could see all the mad cuties waiting on the line. I knew it was going down. They'd already taken a peek at the whip. The rest would be their story.

"Did you see his ride?" I overheard one broad asked another.

"Damn, did you see who's inside?"

There was a buzz on the line as I walked by. The blunt had me lit. I was ready to mingle. There were plenty of nice looking broads, well dressed in their high heels. I vowed to find me sump'n to curl up with through the morning. My mind floated as I walked through the crowd. I spotted them niggas standing off to the side.

"He's here, that nigga Pooh. Whassup baby-boy?" Squeeze almost knocked me over with his hug. His grip steadied me from falling. I was released and then fell into the embrace of Big Show. We hugged for a sec and then I began looking around for Promise.

"Yo, y'all looking sharp," I said. "Where da nigga Promise at?"

"You looking freshly dipped, my nig. Da nigga sez he'll be here." Show said and gave me another dap and hug.

A lot of feelings generated at that moment and I'm sure me seeing Promise would have made it even better. Although it had been only couple weeks, it seemed like months, whatever it was had to be the longest period the four of us hadn't been around each other.

"I had a boy, nigga," Show yelled.

He handed me the fattest blunt I'd ever seen. Godfather size. I stuck it in my pocket and showed him more love. We patted each other's head like we did at the park, when we had swatted someone's lay-up attempt. Show was feeling very good and I know his son would be great at sump'n. We both directed our stares at Squeeze.

"Wha' happen wid you, big Squeeze? Ain't your woman pregnant, she should...?"

"My woman, my baby, I don't know y'all. That bitch probably giving birth to an elephant, I swear. It's been like a year now. The bitch come to me the other day and sez the doctors may have to induce labor and all that bullshit. Got a nigga stressed," Squeeze said and threw his hands up. He reached for a cigarette.

"You're really stressing, dog. Cigarettes? Whassup with that?"

"Can't you tell? A nigga stress, dogs. I got to go down south. When I come back up, we back in bizness, aiight. I need the break from that bitch," Squeeze said. Show and I laughed.

"We waiting on Promise, that nigga called. Sez he was stuck on the LIE. That was about a half hour ago."

"Word, Show?" Squeeze asked.

"Word up," Show said.

"We ain't gotta wait out here, right? Wha' that nigga doing in LI? That nigga bought property out there or sump'n?" I asked jokingly.

"That nigga got this nice looking chick from out there."

"Say word?" I asked incredulously. It was news to me. "That nigga got a girl?"

"Been..." Show said then Squeeze cut him off.

"He's over his baby mom's death and all that emotional shit. Nigga flossin' with some schoolteacher, bitch from out on the island, son. Where've you been? This been going on for a minute now," Squeeze said.

"Yeah, you forgot? I ain't seen y'all in a minute."

"True," Show said mulling it.

"Give me the 411, nigga. Does she have a fatty? Is she a cutey?"

"She's a dime, son and, she's supposed to be bringing her home-girl."

"Oh hmm I got it. That's the reason you're standing out here, huh?"

"Da nigga wants first dibs on da shortie, ahight," Show said jokingly. "I'm a roll up inside this muthafuckin jam wid Pooh, then dogs. I can't wait out here for Promise I don't wanna miss any o' these sexy asses walking round here."

"Man, I ain't waitin' on no first dibs. Y'all know me. Don't act like y'all don't know me."

Squeeze shouted throwing up his arms and popping his collar. He was getting louder with each word just like reverends do, and laying the gospel on real thick on the sinners prior to passing around the plate for the offering.

"Go on and preach," Show said.

"Pass the blunt," Squeeze said and brazenly sparked it.

We strolled down the Ave. puffing the way we used to when we were shorties coming up. Temporary euphoria trailed us colored in marijuana smoke. People all around were tolerant. No one uttered a word to differ, no one complained. No one called the cops. We laughed hard when someone said, "That sure smells like good weed."

We all turned around in time and gazed at an elderly, white couple smiling behind us.

"Want some?" Squeeze offered.

"No thanks, young man. We had our share of pot in our days," the man answered as they moved on.

We were fully bent, when we drifted back to the club. Our reddened, weeded eyes were peeled, looking for Promise in the midst of the downtown party crowd. That nigga was nowhere in sight.

"It's kinda late. I don't know 'bout Promise," Show yelled.

"Hit Promise on the two-way, Squeeze," I said.

"I already did."

"He told me he coming through so…"

"It's going on one o' clock," I said looking at my wrist.

"Be easy, you might blind me you blinging so loud, player," Squeeze said. "I got a little sump'n, sump'n too now." He grabbed the heavy cross of a platinum pendant.

"Ahight, ahight. Who can fuck wid this pinkie diamond ring?"

"Oh, goddamn! You see the ass on that bitch, dogs."

"Yo, so we ready? Let's go in this piece, dogs," I said, still feeling jovial.

We were able to walk right in because Squeeze and Show knew the cat promoting the gig. This was gonna be our new venture; party promotion and club owners. I wasn't gonna let Promise's new attitude affect how I felt. Promise and his new girl could stay out there on the Island.

I didn't give a what! It was good to see Squeeze and Show, I was gonna party. There were still lines of broads waiting to get up in the club. We were escorted through the front entrance. I swear that some female drooled as I went by her. She must have stared too long at my eyes.

Squeeze was talking to his homeboy. Show was up on some other fatty. It gave me time to check out the club. It could be something major. I looked around noticing the amount of nice broads in the place. I'd never guess that we could hold this down. Squeeze was working an angle on doing exactly that. It should be a good look for us.

"Are you seeing these nice asses, Pooh?" It was Squeeze walking up behind me. "We got wait to get up to the VIP," he said. "Where that nigga Show at?"

"I don't know. That nigga just took off with a big-butt-cutie."

"How's the place?" Squeeze asked. He was so hyped whirling his arms that he almost slapped the broad going by him. "I'm sorry ma," he said graciously with that hood charm.

Honey-dip showed her pearly whites. She was a petite Spanish broad with ample boobs. Nice fronts, not bad. I summed them up with quickness. All her friends were equally sexy looking broads.

"Yeah, this place is definitely jumping," I said eyeing the broad with big boobs.

"If you're wondering if they're real? It's okay they real. You don't have to reach out to feel all you have to do is ask I'll show you." She smiled and flashed some thirty six D's then blew us a kiss before she started to walk away, ass shaking.

"Honey, what's your name?" Squeeze yelled after her.

"From the windows to the walls this place is krunked, dog," I said slapping Squeeze high five.

"Yeah! It's gonna be pumping some real dividends real soon, sun. Those same chicks are gonna make it all happen, legit."

"You'll always be a playa, nig."

"You know it, Pooh," Squeeze said. He stood closest to me and judging from the look on his face, I could see he wasn't just talking.

On the streets where a single lesson could cost your life, it was a given that if someone did something, it was either because they'd already done it before and lived through it, or they chilled with someone who had. It was hard to get a person from the street to change their game. It took more than soap and showers to remove the stubborn grime from your mind.

"What's this I hear that new pussy got Promise thinking of settling down, nig?"

"Nah, son, it ain't just a matter of that."

"Nah Squeeze, Promise know, we playas for life."

"Man, its time even I do sump'n else, son. I got my seed on the way…" Squeeze started but I cut him off.

"Yo, but I thought we were family. Blood's thicker than water, dogs. How could Promise just make a decision like that without talking to his peeps? It's like cutting off those who you close wid."

"True but ain't none of us need anyone's permission. I'm a grown man with responsibilities. Promise a grown nigga. Everybody gotta look out for themselves." Show walked over and handed me his cellphone.

"Promise, nig. He said he wanted to holla at you." Show

said. I stared at the cellular like it had germs.

"Man, keep the phone. The music's too loud to hear anything. Is he coming through?"

"Nah," Show said. Squeeze grabbed the phone and walked away.

"Oh, that pussy must be real good for him to just stand up his peeps," I said.

"He sez it ain't just about no pussy, sun." Show said.

"I told you, niggas, Promise got too soft," I said as Squeeze walked back to us.

"Yo, that nigga said he has some problem and ain't gonna make it," Squeeze said.

"Promise knew he wasn't coming from the jump."

"That nigga said his daughter's sick and..."

"You know that he front'n. His seed might not even be ill. He just ain't wanna be here"

"Probably don't wanna even be round us...Fuck it! It is what it is..." Squeeeze began.

"Nah Squeeze, it is what you want it to be," I said looking at his shiny blue gators.

We stood hands in pockets looking each other over then Squeeze said, "I'm gonna holla at my man. He's up in VIP, ahight? He makin' this jump-off a blast. We gon' talk 'bout being silent partners. Peace out," he said moving away, while flashing the peace sign.

"I saw that honey wid da fatty from da building. I'm a go bag that," Show said and both started to walk away from me then stopped. "You takin da walk young un?" Show asked.

"Nah, I'm cool. Ahight, dogs. Go do y'all thing, thing," I said just as two broads walked purposely into me despite me trying to get out of their path. "I'm sorry ma," I said apologetically. Honey dip caught all our eyes and for that moment everyone forgot what they were about to do.

"You too fine to be sorry," one said as they walked by. They were sizzling.

"That guy with the hazel eyes is fine enough to be mine," the other one replied turning back to sneak a peek at me while making sure I heard. Their game was transparent.

"They probably lesbians," Show mused. "They dimes though. Strictly dimes in da building, kid." His broad smile came next. "They look hot. Go get you some o' that, Pooh. They look like they hungry for you."

"They feelin' you, son," Squeeze said, patting my shoulders. I didn't need the encouragement. I was already pushing up on the broads.

"Hey ma, come here sweetness." They walked over to where we stood, holding hands. My dick got rock hard watching them sashay over! I said, "Me and my man here, we wanna see them thongs, sweetness." They both turned around like dancers and shimmied their jeans down just enough for us to feast our eyes. "Hmm looking good, good looking. I'm a come see you later, ma."

"We'll be right over there," they said and walked away. "He's so fine."

"I see you got some girls," Squeeze said.

"Nah, I came here to see my peeps and..."

"Yeah, whatever man. But on da real, I'm going through this process of trying to set some shit done on the legal tip," Squeeze said.

"Word, I was just thinking of that same shizit, dogs. On da

real," I said excitedly.

"Man, you got to get legit. You know in da streets nothing last more than a minute, dogs."

"But we can keep our thing going in da streets, dogs, we..."

Squeeze stopped me in my tracks. Show had walked away and now hurried back carrying drinks. He was excited.

"Her friend is looking real fuck'ble too, dogs. She's too fine for a..." Show's voice trailed off when he saw the grimace on each of our faces. Show looked sharply at Squeeze then me. His head snapped back and forth a few times like he was at a ping pong match and then he said, "What's da fuck is up wid y'all akking like bitches. Come on niggas, this a party, y'all," he said and then turned directly to me. "There's a time and place for everything. Pooh, you ahight, my lil' nig?"

I was disappointed by everything and didn't respond. We all felt a bit let-down but Show still wanted to party.

"Niggas acking up in da club like they got beef wid each other. If you got beef let me know cuz I brought the burner," Show said.

"What you gonna do, Pooh?" Squeeze asked.

"Cause Promise got a teacher from Long Island as his bitch, this nigga acting like I should be kissing his ass."

"Easy, young un," Show said, "Do not disrespect."

"Pooh knows me better than that. If he's gonna dis..." Squeeze started but I cut him off.

"Man, chill. You know I ain't disrespectful but..."

"Yo, Pooh, you smoke some o' that ooh-wee tonight before you left the crib?" Show asked with a huge grin developing on his ugly mug.

"Why you always trying to be funny, huh?" I asked, staring him down.

"You need to calm da fuck down when you talkin' to your elders, nigga," Show said.

"Elders? What? Here's your elders!" I said, grabbing my crotch.

"Man...don't let me..."

"What?"

"You got a little too much tension in you, baby bubba. I ain't too far from taking your ass out in the streets and beating you like you my son."

"Yeah? That's da deal, huh?"

"Yeah nigga, that's whassup. You just be wildin' out too fucking much, young un," Show said taking a couple steps toward me. I didn't flinch. If he wanted he could come get it, I wasn't backing down.

"What? Why you always akking up? You da youngest but you be wanting to bring all this tension wid you," Squeeze said. "It's like you always gotta prove sump'n. Yo man, there is too much tension between us. We gosta chill."

"Yo, this nigga man. he always akking like he gonna bring sump'n..." Show said.

The angst had reached boiling point. "I got sump'n for you," I said, knowing that Show was too big to back down.

"Baby boy, ain't nothing but air between you and me. We can take it to the streets right now, dogs," he said, taking a step forward. Squeeze rushed between us and to stopped him.

"Yo, y'all need to settle this beef outside, ahight? I invited y'all here to chill and have a good time..." Squeeze said.

"Word, dogs, lets chill man. This is a big move for us. We

came to show nothing but l-o-v-e. Why we fighting? You da bad guy or sump'n?" Show laughed and playfully shoved me.

"Yeah, I'll be bad guy cuz I want us to flourish. Go ahead and say it. I ain't going nowhere. These streets belong to me and I don't want to let it go. I'll be that bad guy," I said, shoving him back.

They stared at me like I was infected by the virus. For a minute, it seemed like they were giving me a look of sympathy, then it was as if we were all staring each other down. My anger boiled and I felt like killing sump'n but no guns were drawn. From the looks on our faces, we all knew we were at the crossroads of our relationship. Promise had found himself another love interest and it had destroyed what we had built.

Now it was him, his daughter and some teacher bitch he had recently bagged from Long Island. Squeeze wanted us to lay low. And both he and Show stood by Promise. That left me on the outs.

We were in the club with the music ringing and should have been having a good time. But how do you have a good time when you know everything is over? I walked away.

"Y'all gonna act all funny with a nigga, huh? I don't need y'all. I don't need none y'all," I said.

"Man, lets leave that young un alone. Da nigga's got issues with his mother. He's da brooding type," Show said.

"Let's go up to the VIP lounge and chill wid honey and her friends," Squeeze said. "Hold it down, Pooh. We gonna holla at you later, ahight my nig?" I heard him shout but I didn't hear the whispers.

"That nigga's gonna get his ass kicked again for doin' dumbshit..."

All I knew was I was gonna do me for a minute. I didn't need to be round them niggas tonight. I was man to do what the fuck I wanted. After leaving maduke's home, ain't nobody else left to tell me how to live my life.

The sound of Rakim had most of the partygoers stepping. I flipped my collar searching to find the two Spanish chicks from earlier. They had shown me their thongs and had shown interest. Now they should be ready to get up out of 'em panties.

I paced the club like a bloodhound sniffing for them pair of broads. Party people danced and pranced in time with the rhythm. Everywhere people were screaming while I tried to pick up the scent of my prey.

I saw the big boob broad. She winked and I waved but I wanted that pair of ass on my mind. Big boobs will get a rain-check. The music played and I kept walking. Among the hard-noses flexing up in the club with the wallflowers, I spotted them. The pair was drinking and dancing.

I waved at a waitress and told her to bring the chilliest bottle of Cristal. She told me that due to the high price, I'd have to pay first. She smiled when I pulled out the phat knot.

"I'll be right back," she said still holding that smile.

"I'll be over there," I said pointing to where the girls were.

The Cristal arrived before I did and then it was game time. They were dancing with each other as I approached. I joined right between them pretending to be dancing around but really feeling up on both their asses, sizing them up.

They were both good looking. I wasn't fucking with nothing but dime-pieces. Their caramel tone was set off by jet-black hair. They threw their hands up wildly, playfully flirting along with me. These broads were already two drinks deep and jovial. Tits bounced and waistlines were grinding as the girls displayed the rest of their wares. The Cristal got them sprung. They were about to pop out their thongs. They would get this dick, I thought as I watched them wind their waistlines.

We guzzled drink after drink reveling in the moment. They were what a nigga needed, a distraction to the problem I had with my niggas. I wanted to let my stress off on and two broads would be better than one. A few more drinks and we exitied the club. I staggered a little from the alcohol but I was ahight.

With all the alcohol inside us I watched as the girls skipped to the ride and we piled in. One of the girls was in the back. I reached in the ashtray and lit the clip I had been smoking and then we took off.

"What's your name, playa?" the broad sitting next to me asked.

"They call me Pooh," I said puffing good ganja.

"Are you gonna pass the blunt or what, Pooh?"

"Sure, but why don't you roll up sump'n from scratch?" I asked reaching around.

Her eyes widened when I pulled out the sack of dro. We rode through the city easy in the whip. The broad in the front seat next to me concentrated on rolling up while the other burned a cigarette. They were both cooling. I pumped up the volume on Sleepy Brown in the ride, dropped the top, and we steamed as we glided down East River drive.

"Lets roll over to my place," the broad in the backseat suggested.

"Oh yeah, she just got her new place over there near Flatbush," the broad in the front seat said. It didn't matter where; I'd be fucking sump'n tonight.

"Where in Flatbush?"

"Take the BQE. I'll tell when we're there."

It was early morn and the Beemer zinged through the streets. The breeze of cool air felt refreshing. I raised the roof as the temperature cooled somewhat. The broads were both quiet as the weed and alcohol seeped into their systems. A few minutes later, we pulled up outside her brownstone. She must have been sitting on some cheddar cause the place was dope.

I went inside and the place was mostly unfurnished. There was a bed and a couple chairs. There were no curtains and the windows were so huge, one could see from inside out.

"Make yourself at home, Pooh," one of them called out to me.

I remember reclining on the bed and glancing without caring around the bedroom area. There was no furniture and that made it seem bigger. Nice place, I thought easing back on the empty bed. One of the broads joined me. She brought some coke in a glass vial. She spooned some in her nose and set some off in a pipe. These broads were wild. I watched her wiggle out of her jeans and slipped her thongs out the crack of her ass. I loosened my shirt buttons and flexed in my wife-beater.

"Those jeans were so tight. This is much better," she said walking away. "Do you want sump'n to drink?" she asked casually.

"Yeah," I answered with a smile. "Bring a bottle."

She smiled and walked out. Then the other walked in. She had the red thong and the other wore a black one. It didn't matter, they were both gonna be getting this dick, I thought.

"Where did Ariana go? I thought she was in here with you," she said and then walked back out. I eased around just in time to see two men crashing through the window. I was surprised but instinctively reached for my nine millimeter. I spun and a let off three or four shots hitting one.

"Ugh..." I heard before he fell and the other one started firing back. I returned fire and knew that I had to get to my car.

The .22 was in the ride. I had to get to that. I didn't know how many niggas there were but I knew someone was going to die and I didn't want it to be me. I flicked the light switch off and ran to the door. It did not go completely dark as expected. There was light shining straight through the uncovered windows from the lamp on the street corner.

I tripped over the body of one of the girls. Blood ran over her exposed breasts. She had been shot twice in the chest. Since one of the broads had been shot down, I realized that this wasn't a set up. I had to get up out or die.

No time for my shirt. I didn't want to just run through the door firing with only my wife beater on, but I had to. There had to be about six of them now. I was running out of rounds. I peeped out the front door and fired twice to see from what direction the shooting was coming. Streetlight was limited so it was hard to see.

I heard the scream and gunshots blasted close to my head. I ducked and dove from the door. Bullets went crashing through the door. Someone had a good bead on me. I stayed low and started firing. I figured they had probably killed the other broad and would be coming for me any second.

Caution quickly left. I wasn't familiar with the lay of this crib but I knew the window was near and was the easiest way out. It would surprise them mu'fuckas and then I would be able to get to the whip. I could see my car from where I was.

I waited a few seconds then, as I heard the patter of feet against the floor, I fired a couple a times and jumped out the window rolling. I felt a shard of glass ripping my flesh but I wasn't ready to die and started running toward the whip. As soon as I reached over to open the door, I saw the wires ripped apart from the inside out. The guts of my car were on the floor.

"Fuck these niggas!" I banged the steering wheel. The car was no good. The whole electronic system had been dug-up and left all over the seats. I heard more gunshots.

"He's outside. The nigga went through the window…"

"Get that mu'fucka. Don't let that nigga get away."

Shots zinged recklessly by me. I ran and dialed my cell. No service: Only in Brooklyn. I knew I had to get the fuck out with the quickness and I ran hard. Too late to get a cab and too early to see any bus, I hit the hard top and ran in search of a dollar van.

I waved but most of the drivers thought I was drunk or crazy and swerved to avoid me. I looked back and saw the mu'fuckas' headlights coming after me. I had to keep moving. Just as I was about to try the cell again, they were on me like fiends on a car park on the wrong side of town. These niggas were coming for revenge.

"Yeah, mu'fucka what you gonna do now, nigga?"

There was nothing left to do but high tail it out of the hood and try to make it to my hood alive. I kept it moving. When suddenly in the background, I heard an explosion. They either blew up my car or that broad's beautiful place. I didn't hang around to find out.

I ran as fast as I could and ducked outta site when oncoming headlights blinded me. It was them niggas. Fuck, they had a car. I got up and ran to the busy side of the road trying to find the subway station.

I knew I had been shot when I ran into the station and now I could hear the ambulance siren. I could see paramedics trying desperately to keep my lifeline going.

Lying here on the gurney in the Kings County Emergency Room, I wished there was a point where I could've stopped before reaching this point. I couldn't second-guess but I wished I could have stopped when we were all in the park, kids growing up with everyone sitting around except us.

By then I'd gotten too close to my fam, Squeeze, Promise and Show, to ever think of letting go of the brothers I'd desperately craved. I saw us in the park running, screaming, and stopping every time a gangster walked by.

"That's who I wanna be like."

"Yeah that nigga real cool."

"Out in da streetz, that nigga is da man…" we would argue and make up stories, never worrying about what happens when you die. Who hurts?

I saw them now, hands wringing and heads shaking. All their faces flushed from fighting their tears back. We were just some shorties who came up on the rough do or die turf. If this was my end, no one should shed a tear for me. I'd made my own decisions and lived this gangster life the way I had wanted to. There was no one left to blame, my niggas.

They looked sad and forlorn. Hugging each other again and again, embracing like they never wanted to let go. Anyone could tell that we were truly family and they had come to represent for their fallen brother. There is strength in unity. Every ounce of feeling genuine, here was the camaraderie I always wanted.

Everything was perfect except the fact that my loyal brothers were unable to tell that I knew what was going down with them at the moment. I lay stretched out on this gurney with this scene in my head as I lay dying. The look in their face confirmed the fact that I'd forever be remembered as a gangster. It was a good thing to see the faces of my brothers just before my spirit exited this world.

My body was getting colder and colder, but I could still feel the warmth of their hearts as they drummed for me. Don't mourn me, ride for my memory. I could feel them but images were fading fast. I heard their voices loud and clear.

"We gonna get em, dogs. We got to get them back for baby boy Pooh."

Those words would guarantee my infamy because now there was nothing but love left between my brothers and me. We were as grimy as the gutter that was the blood of our lifeline. It filled our hearts allowing us to dream big and think great thoughts and to execute our plans like a team tailor made for championships.

The streets had nourished us and provided us with a way to support our external family. But in accepting all that, you had to live and die with the contradiction that the streets don't love anyone. The people who stick around to the end, they do. As my physical presence broke down, I could hear the hearts speaking inside my niggas.

"Yeah, we gonna have to get at Nine and his crew. Them muthafuckas killed da young 'un. They deserve to die," Show said with bravery and pride.

"We've got to ride on Nine and rep for Pooh. Don't tell me you're gonna front, Promise. We gotta let em niggas feel us, dogs."

Squeeze exalted the others with his gat ready to explode at the wrong people. 'Nine didn't kill me,' I wanted to yell. It hurt when I realized that no matter how much I screamed they couldn't hear me.

"Yeah, let's ride for Pooh."

Promise's heart wasn't into the streets anymore. He should pull out. He just didn't want the others to think he was a coward. It's all good cuz he had showed mad love by even coming here to see me. That was one thing I never expected. After all this, I wanted so badly to apologize. He had been nothing but a big brother to me and I had murdered his baby-mom.

In one jealous fit of anger, I had pulled the trigger that left her body cold on the sidewalk in front of her apartment building. It was my worse act, I wanted to tell someone and get the weight off my chest, but could never bring myself to doing. How do you tell your brother that you killed his child's mother? I'm so sorry for that evil deed, Promise. All you did was try to show me, your lil' brother some real brotherly love. Instead, I had betrayed you and caused you to suffer.

My heart cried and I wanted to join them hugging each other, especially when I saw their clenched fists. So many things I wanted to say to my peeps. Tell them how they helped me out in this life. My time on earth was up. You don't choose the moment when you die— you just know it will be the wrong time. Sometimes it's your turn and you never know when it will be, you've gotta live your life right. Living fast you will die young.

The look of hope and determination pushed the sadness away from their mugs. They filed out the way we did when we were kids, leaving the classroom heading for the streets, each of us a crutch for the other. I was the youngest and they'd be out there by the school gate waiting to protect me from the bullies. There would be no more waiting. My brothers would be going on without me.

As the doctors poked around, my body got colder and colder and I saw my brothers through a tunnel that kept recessing deeper. I saw their backs and for the moment, a speckle of sunlight came through as the door opened.

It wasn't Nine. I wanted so badly to utter those words, but couldn't. Don't take another man's life endlessly. I was doomed in my failure to communicate the message. My fate was dying and going to the grave, knowing my crew was about to kill the wrong man. This would be the punishment for all my actions. No preacher to forgive my deadly ways. I had lived recklessly fast, now I was dying young and leaving such a good-looking corpse.

With their gloves and the masks peeled off, the men and women in white coats mumbled as they walked out of the emergency room.

"Gosh, there wasn't much we could've done for him. Those bullets caused too much bleeding."

"I guess he's reached the end of his ride, anyway."

"What a waste, he was such a good looking guy. Well, it's

time for my break."

"I guess it's my turn to fill out the report and notify his next of kin."

Sadness closed the window from which my spirit departed. My body wrapped tightly captured and frozen in eternal darkness. Maybe I tried but I would have to die knowing the feeling I will not be able to rid myself of what's trapped in my subconscious mind. Forever, existing inside my soul.

The lights seem dimmer. Coldness froze my veins. No more pain, no strain and that could only mean one thing. I have reached the limit in this life and therefore it must be the end. Lord, forgive me for all my sins...

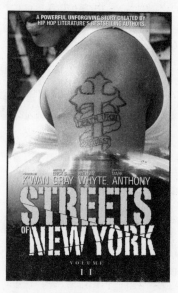

Street of New York
Volume II

ERICK S GRAY

Known as Mr. Prolifick, this young and very talented storyteller is honing his skills as a legend in the book game. He's written classics such as the exciting erotica, Booty Call *69 and the best fiction and award winning, gangster saga, Crave All... Lose All. Hailing from South Side. Jamaica, Queens, Mr. Prolifick goes hard for his on the STREETS OF NEW YORK.

Hit up Erick S Gray at www.streetlitreview.com

ANTHONY WHYTE

He's the master of this literary domain, holding the book game down like it was his kingdom. Author of the classic, Ghetto Girls Series, editor and CEO of Augustus Publishing, the hottest on the book scene. A true pioneer and leader, Whyte's style has been copied never duplicated. He's way ahead of his time. In grand steeze, he continues to reign. Since '96 when he coined the phrase, Hip Hop Literature, Whyte has been forever bringing reading back to real life.

Hit up Anthony Whyte at www.streetlitreview.com

MARK ANTHONY

The author and publisher is a talented veteran of the book game. Reppin' Q-Boro, the publishing house he started and the area he's from. Mark Anthony has conquered the publishing world while writing several stories of grit and grime... from Paper Chasers to Ladies' Nite, his style definitely appeals to readers of all sex, especially to the ladies.

Hit up Mark Anthony at www.streetlitreview.com

WHERE
HIP-HOP
LITERATURE
BEGINS...

AUGUSTUS PUBLISHING

Augustus Publishing was created to unify minds with entertaining, hard-hitting tales from a hood near you. Hip Hop literature interprets contemporary times and connects to readers through shared language, culture and artistic expression. From street tales and erotica to coming-of age sagas, our stories are endearing, filled with drama, imagination and laced with a Hip Hop steez.

GHETTO GIRLS IV
Young Luv
ESSENCE BESTSELLING AUTHOR ANTHONY WHYTE

Ghetto Girls IV Young Luv
$14.95 // 9780979281662

Ghetto Girls
$14.95 // 0975945319

Ghetto Girls Too
$14.95 // 0975945300

Ghetto Girls 3 Soo Hood
$14.95 // 0975945351

THE BEST OF THE STREET CHRONICLES TODAY, THE **GHETTO GIRLS SERIES** IS A WONDERFULLY HYPNOTIC ADVENTURE THAT DELVES INTO THE CONVOLUTED MINDS OF CRIMINALS AND THE DARK WORLD OF POLICE CORRUPTION. YET, THERE IS SOMETHING THRILLING AND SURPRISINGLY TENDER ABOUT THIS ONGOING YOUNG-ADULT SAGA FILLED WITH MAD FLAVA.

Love and a Gangsta
author // **ERICK S GRAY**

This explosive sequel to **Crave All Lose All**. Soul and America were together ten years 'til Soul's incarceration for drugs. Faithfully, she waited four years for his return. Once home they find life ain't so easy anymore. America believes in holding her man down and expects Soul to be as committed. His lust for fast money rears its ugly head at the same time America's music career takes off. From shootouts, to hustling and thugging life, Soul and his man, Omega, have done it. Omega is on the come-up in the drug-game of South Jamaica, Queens. Using ties to a Mexican drug cartel, Omega has Queens in his grip. His older brother, Rahmel, was Soul's cellmate in an upstate prison. Rahmel, a man of God, tries to counsel Soul. Omega introduces New York to crystal meth. Misery loves company and on the road to the riches and spoils of the game, Omega wants the only man he can trust, Soul, with him. Love between Soul and America is tested by an unforgivable greed that leads quickly to deception and murder.

$14.95 // 9780979281648

A POWERFUL UNFORGIVING STORY
CREATED BY HIP HOP LITERATURE'S BESTSELLING AUTHORS

THIS THREE-VOLUME KILLER STORY FEATURING FOREWORDS FROM
SHANNON HOLMES, K'WAN & **TREASURE BLUE**

Streets of New York vol. 1
$14.95 // 9780979281679

Streets of New York vol. 2
$14.95 // 9780979281662

Streets of New York vol. 3
$14.95 // 9780979281662

AN EXCITING, ENCHANTING... A FUNNY, THRILLING AND EXHILARATING
RIDE THROUGH THE ROUGH NEIGHBORHOODS OF THE GRITTY CITY. THE MOST FUN YOU
CAN LEGALLY HAVE WITHOUT ACTUALLY LIVING ON THE STREETS OF NEW YORK. READ
THE STORY FROM HIP HOP LITERATURE TOP AUTHORS:

ERICK S. GRAY, MARK ANTHONY & ANTHONY WHYTE

Lipstick Diaries Part 2
A Provocative Look into the Female Perspective
Foreword by **WAHIDA CLARK**

Lipstick Diaries II is the second coming together of some of the most
unique, talented female writers of Hip Hop Literature. Featuring a
feast of short stories from today's top authors. **Genieva Borne, Camo,
Endy, Brooke Green, Kineisha Gayle, the queen of hip hop lit; Carolyn
McGill, Vanessa Martir, Princess Madison, Keisha Seignious,** and a
blistering foreword served up by the queen of thug love; Ms. **Wahida
Clark.** Lipstick Diaries II pulls no punches, there are no bars hold
leaves no metaphor unturned. The anthology delivers a knockout with
stories of pain and passion, love and virtue, profit and gain, ... all told
with flair from the women's perspective. Lipstick Diaries II is a

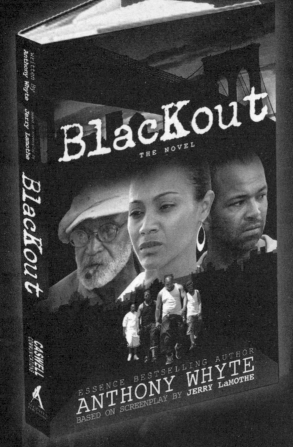

The lights went out
and the
mayhem began.

It's gritty in the city but hotter in Brooklyn where a small community in east Flatbush must come to grips with its greatest threat, self-destruction. August 14 and 15, 2003, the eastern section of the United States is crippled by a major shortage of electrical power, the worst in US history. Blackout, the spellbinding novel is based on the epic motion picture, directed by Jerry Lamothe. A thoroughly riveting story with delectable details of families caught in a harsh 48 hours of random violent acts, exploding in deadly conflict. There's a message in everything... even the bullet. The author vividly places characters on the stage of life and like pieces on a chess-board, expertly moves them to a tumultuous end. Voila! Checkmate, a literary triumph. Blackout is a masterpiece. This heart-stopping, page-turning drama is moving fast. Blackout is destined to become an American classic.

BASED ON SCREENPLAY BY JERRY LaMOTHE

Inspired by true events

US $14.95 CAN $20.95
ISBN 978-0-9820653-0-3

CASWELL
COMMUNICATIONS

ENJOY THE MOST EXHILARATING RIDE THROUGH HIP HOP LITERATURE
CHECK OUT THESE PREVIOUS RELEASES FROM AUGUSTUS PUBLISHING

ipstick Diaries
author // VARIOUS AUTHORS
$14.95 // 0975945394

A Boogie Down Story
author // KEISHA SEIGNIOUS
$14.95 // 0979281601

Crave All Lose All
author // ERICK S GRAY
$14.95 // 097928161X

If It Ain't One Thing It's Another
author // SHARRON DOYLE
$14.95 // 097594536X

Woman's Cry
author // VANESSA MARTIR
$14.95 // 0975945386

Booty Call *69
author // ERICK S GRAY
$14.95 // 0975945343

A Good Day To Die
author // JAMES HENDRICKS
$14.95 // 0975945327

Spot Rushers
author // BRANDON McCALLA
$14.95 // 0979281628

t Can Happen n a Minute
author // S.M. JOHNSON
$14.95 // 0975945378

Hustle Hard
author // BLAINE MARTIN
$14.95 // 0979281636

ORDER INFO
Mail us a list of the titles you would like and
$14.95 per Title + shipping charges **$3.95** for
one book & **$1.00** for each additional book.
Make all checks payable to:
Augustus Publishing 33 Indian Rd. NY, NY 10034
Email: info@augustuspublishing.com

Bookstores & Distributors contact:
Publishers Group West | www.pgw.com
Customer Service 800-788-3123
1700 Fourth Street Berkeley, California 94710

AugustusPublishing.com

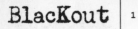

BlacKout

THE NOVEL

ESSENCE BESTSELLING AUTHOR
ANTHONY WHYTE
BASED ON SCREENPLAY BY **JERRY LaMOTHE**

Enjoy this Excerpt from BlacKout the Novel

ONE

August 14, 2003, 8:00 a.m.

The people of Flatbush, Brooklyn awoke to the sweltering heat coming off the top of the apartment buildings. Sunshine and high humidity locked the city in a ferocious heat vice. Craving relief, the residents of Browser Street migrated from their apartments to enjoy the fresh air outdoors.

It was around 9 a.m. when three women of West Indian descent sat on lawn chairs blocking the entrance to 254 Browser Street. They were busy chatting up the latest gossip, while keeping their eyes on the crowd of teens surrounding Tech. He was in front of the barbershop hawking his CDs and DVDs.

"I got it all," Tech shouted. "From the latest Fifty to classic Biggie, some new Jay-Z, I got it ... I got it!"

By 10:00 a.m., Corey was on his way to the barbershop to get a haircut, and stepped to Tech with a request.

"What it do? You have the new *Bad Boys II* soundtrack?" Corey asked checking out Tech's display.

"I got it right here, dog!" Tech said handing the CD to Corey.

"That joint's bananas," Tech added as Corey examined the disk. "It's selling like crack all day long, everyday," Tech said pushing his sales pitch.

"Hmm…word? What it do?" Corey asked.

"On n' poppin'! Cop it. It's jumpin'. And you need this Sean Paul remix and the G-Unit and Fifty Cent joint… Fire!" Tech said placing two CDs in Corey's hand.

"Ahight, I hear you," Corey said looking at each CD and quickly passing a twenty dollar bill to Tech.

"And I got the new Freddy versus Jason on DVD, director's cut! Fire! What you know about that?"

"Damn! That joint ain't due out for another couple weeks," Corey said scratching his head, visibly impressed.

"What's my muthafucking name, dog?" Tech asked.

"Ahight, you do what ya do, dogs," Corey said smiling and giving Tech a pound.

Nelson and Rick lifted the gate to the barbershop, triggering a sudden flight of pigeons from their overnight perches.

"Whew, its gonna be a mother of a hot one today. You feel the heat already?" Nelson observed, shielding his eyes and gazing at the bright sun.

"Yeah, no doubt. I'm sayin' my brother, may we shine like the sun," Rick nodded in agreement. "Hope we get a lot of heads today," he added walking inside and dusting off his barber chair.

"What it do?" Corey greeted, walking into the barbershop. "I need a fresh one for the weekend, Rick," he continued, taking a seat in Rick's chair and glancing at the mirror.

The barbershop was the place where everyone who was anyone came to hang out. From the latest cuts to freshest style, anything that was popping happened first at Nelson's barbershop.

Nelson was a proud, thirty-something entrepreneur who owned the barbershop. A vocal leader, he had street savvy with genuine social conscience. He was known to stand up for friends and often went out of his way to give a helping hand. At the same time, Nelson had old-school swagger and was known to get down with his knuckle game. He made his reputation fighting for what he believed in.

Rick, one of Nelson's barbers, was also in his thirties and had the rep of being an entertaining brother. Known for his sometimes arrogant ways, Rick enjoyed yapping about his sexual exploits. His different baby mothers would sometimes show up at the barbershop bringing drama. Most of the customers just laughed at his calamities, while he busily laced another satisfied customer with the latest fresh haircut.

Cam was the only female hanging in the group. She was a star athlete in high school, renowned for her basketball prowess. Her talent on the court earned her mad respect from the fellas. She wasn't at the barbershop for haircuts; it was simply her favorite hangout. Not only did Cam enjoy hanging with them, she also dressed like one of the guys, sporting baggy jeans, T-shirt and corn rows.

"Damn, look at the ass on shortie in that video! She doin' what she do," Corey said pointing to the television screen.

For a few rump-shaking seconds, all eyes turned to look at the latest Jigga video playing on BET.

"You know I heard them chicks don't make a dime, shaking ass in those videos, you feeling me?" Nelson announced.

"I don't know about all that. I know they gotta to be eating. I used to date one of'em video-hos, I mean 'chicks', and I'm sayin', the bitch was getting paid," Rick said smiling.

"Yeah, video-ho is right. They getting paid for their services off camera, that's what's really up," Cam said sucking her teeth.

"Sounds a little like hatin', you feel me, Cam?" Nelson smirked.

"Please, I don't love 'em ho's. I likes me a gangsta bitch. I like'em pretty but gangsta, that's what's up," Cam smiled.

"Damn, I'm sayin', you might as well just date a dude," Rick said with a chuckle.

Cam's explanation was drowned by raucous laughter. She resigned herself to throwing up her two middle fingers.

Tech took a break from hustling and walked into the barbershop. He and Nelson were very good friends and shared much history. Both had played on the same high school basketball team and came up hustling drugs with each other. After getting caught up with the law, they both got out the game.

Besides selling mixed CDs, Tech also functioned as the manager for budding rapper L. Tech not only assisted with sales and marketing of his new CD, he was also helping to get L signed to a recording deal with a major label. Tech worked at a friend's makeshift recording studio on Flatbush Avenue and was able to print a couple thousand CDs and sell them. The partnership was going well, but L needed to manage his time better. This is where Tech's help was crucial.

"Where's your boy L? He ain't here yet?" Tech asked Nelson.

"How long have you known L?" Nelson shot back.

"A while now," Tech answered with a chuckle.

"You know that nigga in the bodega messing with them Arabs, or rollin' up sump'n to smoke, " Nelson said.

"That's one hun'red. L's probably at the bodega gettin' a Dutch or sump'n," Tech said.

"You feel me? He does nothing but roll up, gettin' high on bullshit all day long," Nelson laughed.

"He'll be here soon, high as a muthafucka, talking plenty shit. And that's one hun'red," Tech laughed.

The two men exchanged dap like friends who had shared many years of private jokes between them, and Tech went back to work.

"Come get these CDs," Tech shouted to passersby while looking out for L.

21

AUGUSTUS
PUBLISHING